Madeline S
Part Two, v

She slid across t. ... squeeze close to Cal's side.

Their thighs converged, hip to knee, bringing her barely-there stockings into contact with his denim-clad leg. A rush of heat blazed through her making her more determined to seduce this bad boy.

She whispered softly in his ear, "Don't I get a second-date kiss?"

He refused to meet her hot gaze.

She grazed her lips against the scratch of his cheek, stole a quick taste of his warm skin.

He let out a low whistle. "Honey, you don't know what that does to me."

"I wish it did more."

He turned to her suddenly. "Do you mean that, or are you just tempting the hell out of me as some kind of social experiment?"

"I want you, Cal." Maddy trailed a fingertip down his cheek. "I want to see how fast we can go from zero to sixty in that back seat of yours."

Dear Reader,

What good girl doesn't occasionally dream of letting her inner wild woman run free? If you've ever entertained the idea of really letting your hair down, I bet you'll like reading about sociology scholar Madeline Watson, who can't wait to undertake the study of human mating rituals for her dissertation. Too bad the university thinks upstanding Madeline has spent too much time in the ivory tower to undertake such an earthy subject. Now she needs to shed her good-girl image in a hurry, and she knows just the man to help her!

I hope you enjoy seeing how Madeline leads the campus on a steamy, wild ride that turns their lives upside down. *Learning Curves* is set at my alma mater, the University of Louisville in Kentucky. Although I didn't have *quite* as much fun there as Maddy does, I loved every minute spent at that venerable institution in pursuit for my master's degree.

If you like *Learning Curves*, don't miss my first Harlequin Blaze title in February 2002, *Silk, Lace & Videotape*. Visit me at www.JoanneRock.com to learn more about my future releases or to let me know what you thought of my story. I'd love to hear from you!

Happy Reading!

Joanne Rock

LEARNING CURVES
Joanne Rock

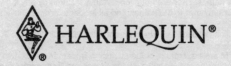

HARLEQUIN®

TORONTO • NEW YORK • LONDON
AMSTERDAM • PARIS • SYDNEY • HAMBURG
STOCKHOLM • ATHENS • TOKYO • MILAN • MADRID
PRAGUE • WARSAW • BUDAPEST • AUCKLAND

To Dean, for ensuring we've always taken
the road less traveled. Thank you for the adventure!

ISBN 0-373-25963-8

LEARNING CURVES

Copyright © 2002 by Joanne Rock.

Printed in U.S.A.

1

"IF YOU'RE FREE Saturday night, would you mind initiating me in the rites of womanhood?"

Thunking herself on the forehead, Madeline Watson slumped down on a bench outside the business department's faculty lounge to wait for her quarry. All the come-on lines she concocted were too stuffy. Head in her hands, she stared down at her penny loafers and wished she'd paid more attention when other women discussed their dating adventures. Why had she spent the past ten years with her nose buried in books? She had no idea how one went about propositioning the sexiest man in town—or any man for that matter.

Wouldn't it be simpler to invest in a killer red dress and a pair of stiletto heels?

She cleared her throat and tried again. "What would you think of taking our relationship to the next level?" A nearby giggle alerted her to the new wave of students tromping through the University of Louisville's echoing marble corridors on their way to evening classes. Great. All Madeline needed to cap off this hideous day was to have a student report her for trying to pick up imaginary men in the hallway.

The embarrassment would be well worth it if her proposition worked, however. No man had ever sent her hormones into overdrive the way Cal Turner could with one lazy smile.

The door to the faculty lounge swung wide and Madeline plastered her back to the wall as if she could root herself to that very spot. A handful of university professors poured through the door, balancing heavy textbooks, steaming cups of coffee and overstuffed briefcases. Their sudden appearance forced Madeline to recall that the object of her quest was no imaginary male. Cal Turner might look like a fantasy, but those drool-worthy pecs were as real as the grading curve.

Madeline rose, praying she wouldn't lose her nerve to face the lone man who would be left in the lounge in a few minutes. She nodded to the handful of professors she knew from her years on staff as a graduate assistant, but most of the coffee-clutching crowd was business faculty, a breed far removed from the social sciences department that Madeline called home.

The old Mae West line ran through her head as she waited. "How'd you like to come up and see me sometime?" But that one didn't really apply to her...she lived in a one-story house just outside of downtown.

She needed something modern. Something direct and aggressive to go along with her quest to be more daring. If she was ever going to get the dissertation review committee to sanction her study of human mating rituals, she had to prove to them there was more to her than just a buttoned-up intellectual. A fling with the most notorious ladies' man on campus ought to do the trick.

The fact that a fling would also fulfill her secret desire for Cal was purely coincidental. Could she help it if the perfect man for the job happened to be someone she fantasized about on a regular basis?

Madeline unbuttoned the top button of her oversize men's shirt and took a deep breath. She could do this.

Once the noise had died down and her digital watch flashed 6:01 p.m., she eased open the frosted-glass door and stepped inside the faculty's inner sanctum. Foam cups littered all three round tables, along with leftover napkins and doughnut crumbs. The only person left in the faculty lounge was Cal.

For a moment Madeline gave in to the pure pleasure of staring at the man who didn't know he held her future in his calloused hands. Seated in a back corner with his elbows on the table, he wore a gray T-shirt depicting the school's mascot—a Louisville Cardinal. The T-shirt stretched over mouth-watering muscles, making him look more like the mechanic he used to be than the successful entrepreneur and business instructor he'd become. Of course, Tuesdays weren't his night to teach. He usually came to the university to review lesson plans and read student papers, even after long days of overseeing his chain of car repair shops, Perfect Timing.

Madeline savored the broad lines of his shoulders, the intriguing cut of sinewy forearms. When she reached his solemn profile, she was unsettled by the chiseled jaw and sharp angles of his face. Without his customary grin, Cal looked less like her good-natured friend and more like the campus wolf.

Perhaps he heard the catch in her breath.

He turned from his grade book. "Hey, gorgeous."

He smiled the killer smile that had probably broken hearts from Cincinnati to Nashville.

Madeline hadn't known knees truly could knock until that moment. What had she been thinking to come here like this? She closed her eyes to steel herself, knowing she'd lose her nerve if she didn't ask him right off the bat.

He waited patiently, his hazel eyes turning her knocking knees to something more akin to jiggling Jell-O.

Don't talk like a textbook, she schooled herself. Act casual.

"I know you're busy and all, Cal." She gulped for air and courage, her heart pummeling her chest in a fit of rebellious nerves. "But what would you say to getting out of here and setting the sheets on fire back at my place?"

For one painfully endless moment, the words hung there, echoing over and over in Madeline's mind.

She slapped her hand over her mouth in a vain attempt to staunch the stupid question she'd already voiced. She lowered her hand, ready to flee if only her feet would cooperate.

Cal blinked back at her, silent. Slowly he closed the grading book in front of him, as if hoping to stall his response.

She hadn't known a moment of such keen mortification since she—the scientist's daughter—had flunked twelfth-grade physics.

"I think all those years on the Harley have started to affect my hearing." He flashed her a rueful grin, complete with the dimple that sent female coeds into swoon mode. "Could you run that by me again?"

There wasn't a chance she would repeat that hideous proposition. "It was nothing really, I—" Unsure what to say, she shuffled backward. "I'm just going to head on back to my building now." She inched further away, eager to escape and disgusted with herself for losing her nerve at the same time.

"Wait a minute." He rose from the chair.

Maybe, if she had been in the company of an average man, Madeline would have made a break for the door. Instead she could only stand there and gape at six-feet-plus inches of impressive male.

He took full advantage of her immobility as he sauntered over to her. Did he know how disarming that dimple could be?

"I thought I heard a very interesting offer just now." A hint of backwoods Tennessee still softened an occasional vowel, lending his words a pleasing drawl.

She shook her head so hard her glasses rattled against her nose. "All those years on the Harley, remember?"

"Maddy, how long have we been friends?" He reached up to cup her shoulders, holding her at arm's length.

Heat stole through her at the contact. "Four years and two months." She recalled every time they'd touched during that time, too. And none of those idle brushes of hands exchanging coffee mugs could compare to the way he held her now. Cal's undivided attention intoxicated her.

"That sounds about right." He looked thoughtful for

a moment. "And during those four years and two months, I have heard you ask me about my garages, my lesson plans, my teaching ideology, and maybe a time or two about my students. But in all that time, not once have you asked me back to your place to set the sheets on fire."

Heat suffused her cheeks, her limbs, her chest... she'd bet even her fingertips were blushing bright red. Obviously he'd heard her question just fine.

"The funny part is, I used to flirt outrageously with you just to get you to crack a smile." He cradled her cheek with one palm and lifted her chin.

Heady sensation clouded her brain cells. She'd had a boyfriend or two since high school, but the emphasis had been on "friend" and those relationships hadn't compared remotely to this. Ever since she'd come to the university, she'd been absorbed in her work, obsessed with succeeding in the academic world and following in her father's footsteps. There'd been no time for a man—until now.

His hand slid away, landing on her shoulder once again. "But no matter how much I teased you, you always turned me down cold."

She blinked up at him, more tongue-tied than usual around Louisville's bad boy. She might be able to quote complex sociological theory and speak in front of a lecture hall full of hundreds of students, but she had no clue how to converse with a man on an intimate level.

"So why don't you explain to me what's going on?" He maneuvered her toward the office chair at the lounge's lone computer terminal, then gently pushed her into the seat. Pulling over another chair, he plunked down in front of her and waited.

Maddy sighed. "I guess that means no?"

There was something unbearably sad about having your best friend turn you down, even though Cal surely had no idea he rated as the closest friend she'd ever had. He probably had other people off campus who were more important in his life with his chain of garages, but Madeline's world of geeky scholars and tenure-obsessed assistant professors brightened whenever Cal was around. She valued the evenings they'd sit together comparing problematic students, the demands of the administration, the joys of the classroom.

Cal lifted his hand to tuck a stray strand of hair behind her ear. "It means that if the Lady Scholar is propositioning a guy from the wrong side of the tracks like me, then her world has obviously been turned upside down. So out with it."

The soft scrape of his fingers against her cheek imparted a pleasure that went far beyond the thrills she found in a successful day of research. Cal's work-roughened hands, the same ones that had wrestled blowtorches and solder guns, caressed her so gently.

Yet she knew that physical pleasure was only temporary, even if she'd never fully experienced it before. Her career field—sociological studies—had always been the one constant in her life. She had to find a way to get her project approved. If only Cal would help.

Cal watched Madeline take deep breaths. She was an odd bird, his Lady Scholar, but he'd had the hots for her since laying his hands on her engine and his eyes on her up-tipped nose four years ago. Intelligent, diligent, and already respected for her contributions to the sociology department even at her young age, Maddy embodied the qualities he most admired in a person.

The fact that she also epitomized the absentminded professor only added to her appeal. Cal guessed she had miles of dark hair, even though she wore it in some sort of knot all the time. She seemed to have no clue she was gorgeous—in a sweet, unassuming way. Cal wondered sometimes if he was the only guy on campus who recognized it. Maddy trooped around the university in sensible shoes and glasses, her delicate figure hidden beneath her bulky men's clothing.

Cal had passed many pleasurable hours imagining precisely what that body looked like beneath those baggy shirts. Like a car cover over a vintage Vette, her clothes kept her hidden. But Cal had always been able to spot a classic, even when shrouded. She'd put up with enough of his come-ons to last her through her next two degrees and hadn't once bitten. What was her game now?

"Honey, I'm not leaving until you tell me what's going on here, so you might as well spill it."

He got up to get her a cup of coffee while she pulled herself together. This had become part of their ritual on Tuesday nights—kicking back in the lounge near his office, sharing java and tales from the classroom. Cal enjoyed shaking off the blue-collar world of his car repair shops with some academic talk, but not nearly as much as he liked being near Maddy. He'd always flirted with her, but now he accepted the friendship she offered. He was safer with friendship anyway, considering his history with relationships.

Friendship he could handle. According to his ex-wife, it was the serious, intimate relationships he screwed up.

Willing away unhappy memories, he returned with two mugs to find Maddy's eyes were bright with unshed tears. She didn't look sad exactly. She looked...furious.

"They turned down my dissertation!" She wailed the words as if she'd announced Armageddon.

"I'm sorry." What did that have to do with her sheet-burning plea? This woman had just flipped his world and now she wanted to talk about her research?

"The dissertation committee wants me to continue my work in literary sociology, but I'm not interested in that anymore." She removed her glasses and pressed the heels of her hands against her forehead.

Cal felt a moment of triumph to see her wide, dark eyes without their perpetual tortoiseshell screen. He folded her glasses and set them aside. "You've had a lot of success in that arena, right?"

"Yes, but I'm ready to move on. I got into sociology because I wanted to study people, not literary theory. I want to do a pure sociological study."

What was it about her stuffy way of speaking that acted like a hormone shot in the arm? The way those luscious lips wrapped around lofty concepts proved brains and beauty could coexist quite happily. "Okay. What did you propose?" He steeled himself for more of her highbrow speak by taking a long swig of coffee.

"I want to study human mating rituals."

It took every bit of control he possessed to not spew

coffee on her shoes. Instead, he opted to choke down his drink and indulge in a long coughing spell.

"Are you okay?" she asked, hammering him on the back with a surprisingly strong fist.

"I don't know," he rasped. "I think you're just taking me a little by surprise today."

She stiffened. "You don't think I'm cut out for it, either, do you?"

"What?" Dear Lord, he'd barely recovered his breath. He wasn't ready for round two.

"You don't think I'm the kind of woman who knows enough about the mating process to write effectively about it." She stood, all five and a half feet of her trembling with anger and indignation.

"Is that what your review committee said?" No wonder she was upset.

She seemed to lose a bit of her edge then, sinking back down into the chair, defeated. "Just because I don't go out very much doesn't mean I can't see mating rituals all around me. It's not like I don't have...feelings."

Thank goodness his coffee cup remained firmly planted on the table, where he intended to leave it for the rest of this conversation. "Just where have you been hanging out to witness these...whatever you call them...'mating rituals'?" Cal didn't know if he'd be able to continue this discussion if they kept flinging around the term "mating."

"I don't mean the sex act," she informed him. "I mean the flirtation that goes on between men and women as a prelude to sex. The human equivalent of mating calls. You know." She waved her hand in the air as if he would understand exactly what she meant. "Mating rituals."

Heat surged through him. He couldn't sit there staring back at her any longer, so he got up and paced the lounge. "This is what you want to study for your dissertation?"

"I want to do some empirical research on what sorts of flirtation leads to an actual relationship."

Cal wiped a hand over his face. "*Now* you mean the sex act."

She beamed at him like a star pupil. "Exactly."

"Won't this be difficult to follow up on?" No wonder her plan had gotten turned down by the review committee. If there had been any men on that board, they wouldn't have been able to sit still through her risqué proposal. "I mean, how will you know what takes place between men and women after they leave your field of vision?"

"Interviews." She sipped her coffee, appearing more calm now that they were discussing her field.

He, on the other hand, felt edgier than a caged beast. "I see."

But he didn't see. All he could envision was naive Madeline Watson camping out at area singles bars in her glasses and sensible shoes, getting hit on by the hounds that hang out in those places. She might be a smart lady when it came to college, but she had obviously lived a sheltered life. She didn't know anything about the world Cal had grown up in—a world where guts and determination counted for more than any degree.

She set her coffee mug back on the table and traced

the red U of L logo with an idle finger. "One of the members of the dissertation committee implied I didn't get approved because I'm not experienced enough to handle such a racy project. Can you imagine?"

That had been his thought exactly. How could you write about flirtation when you'd never tried it? He, of all people, knew Madeline Watson wasn't the type of woman a guy could trade sexual innuendos with. He'd gotten the impression that because her father had been a single parent and a brilliant scientist to boot, Maddy had been a little overprotected.

"But I've decided I'm not going to take no for an answer."

"What do you mean?"

"I'm going to repropose the project." She looked up at him, her gaze unusually sure and steady. "But first, I'm going to procure some of the experience the committee seems to think I'm lacking."

Cal paused in mid-pace and sank onto one of the tables for support. "You're going to procure experience?" He had that feeling you get when they're reading off the lottery numbers and you have them all right so far. Did the Lady Scholar really want to use him for...practice? He couldn't decide whether to be insulted or excited as hell.

"Yes." She stood, her back straight beneath her bulky men's dress shirt.

Still, he could see her fingers pluck a nervous rhythm against the cuff of an overly long sleeve.

"But I need to create a public splash as I do this experience gathering. I need to have an affair that will be highly visible."

Damn. Maddy's public splash was dousing cold water over a scheme that had started out sounding so promising. He couldn't afford a high-visibility affair. Not anymore. "And you were coming to me with this proposal because...?"

Maybe part of him wanted to hear that she'd found something to admire in him after all this time. Underneath that proper exterior, did Madeline Watson hide a small flame for the garage mechanic?

"I came to you because you've got the most notorious reputation on campus. If I'm seen so much as walking to class with you, my status as the inexperienced bookworm with nothing to do on Saturday nights will disappear. And if, perhaps, you imparted a passionate public kiss or two..."

Cal's insides twisted. She only wanted him because his bad reputation might rub off on her. She wanted the man he once was, not the man he was trying to become—the man he *had* to be if he had any hopes of gaining custody of his sister.

Even so, he would have jumped all over that offer a few months ago. He'd have given anything to see what happened when uptight Madeline decided to take a walk on the wild side. If her actions tonight were any indication of what was in store, then it sounded pretty damn enticing to him.

But Madeline officially ranked as a graduate student at U of L, even though she taught more classes than he did. Relations between graduate students and teachers—including part-time ones such as Cal—were frowned upon by the administration. Cal couldn't risk the potential scandal of a relationship like that right now. He was sort of surprised Maddy would, considering her dedication to her job. This project obviously meant a lot to her.

Madeline studied him intently, the flicking rhythm of her fingers against her shirt cuff picking up pace. "Will you help me?"

Cal closed his eyes, knowing he would damn himself for a long time to come. "I'm sorry, Maddy. I can't."

He was prepared for her to be disappointed. He wasn't prepared for the horror in her voice as she echoed his words back at him.

"Can't? What do you mean, you *can't?*"

2

SHOCKED AT CAL'S announcement, Madeline allowed her gaze to roam over the broad expanse of his impressive chest. "I have a hard time believing that, Cal Turner. You have the most notorious reputation on campus! I don't think you could have claimed such a distinction without being perfectly capable of fulfilling the mating function."

Cal's jaw dropped as he gaped at her. "I *am* capable, Maddy." He squeezed his temples, his closed jaw now flexing in what appeared to be a case of vast frustration. "In fact, I am more than capable."

An odd flash of relief sizzled through her at that news. Her quest to study mating rituals aside, she recognized that she had propositioned Cal because she'd been attracted to him for years.

His hands fell to his sides and he stalked toward her. There was no other way to describe how he zeroed in on her as he approached. Like a watchdog with hackles raised, Cal seemed to have flexed every muscle in his possession. She could pick out the lines of virtually every one exposed to her view.

Madeline swallowed hard, trying to will away thoughts of the strong sinews that were off limits to her hungry gaze. Her interest in him wasn't purely carnal, after all. She might have always been attracted to Cal, but she never would have approached him if she hadn't desperately needed his help for scientific purposes.

He didn't stop until he stood toe to toe with her—until his big chest hovered inches from her starched shirt. Her flesh tingled and tightened in direct response to the heat of his body.

"I am also very ready, and physically willing." Cal's hazel eyes seemed to darken to almost-brown as he stared down at her. "Do you know what that means?"

Madeline forced herself to not look down. "I have a pretty good idea."

"The problem is not that I *can't*, Professor, but that I will not allow myself to indulge in..." His gaze slid from her eyes to her body, and perused her with aching slowness. "...the pleasure."

Awareness kicked to life, making her wish for the first time that she was the kind of woman who wore silks instead of cottons. Would he have taken her up on her proposition then?

"Oh." The edgy hunger inside her started to fade—a little anyway—as it began to sink in that he was really telling her no. She took a deep breath and attempted to smile politely. "I see."

"No. You don't see." Cal stepped back a pace and seated himself on one of the tables.

Madeline had no desire to hear Cal's excuses for not sleeping with her. She'd put herself on the line and he'd turned her down flat. She wouldn't stick around for a let's-still-be-friends speech.

"That's okay." She retrieved her glasses and shoved them back where they belonged. Picking up her U of L mug, she retreated to the lounge's small kitchen area. As she washed the cup and placed it back on the rack next to a dozen other people's mugs, she rambled. "I just happened to think of you because we've been friends for a while, and I thought you were safe."

Maddy noticed Cal wince, so she hastened on "But I guess it was a pretty bold thing of me to even ask. Especially since the university could officially ax us if we went too public with a relationship." The administration frequently overlooked liaisons of that sort, but Madeline knew better than to risk her job, didn't she? The whole idea had been crazy—a lame-brained attempt to fulfill a fantasy and to show her review committee she wasn't such an inexperienced old maid after all. She tried to edge past him to the door. "I'd better get back to work now."

"Maddy, wait." He reached out to her, cupping a hand around each of her upper arms.

She wanted to keep on walking. But some emotion in his eyes proved even more compelling than his touch.

Madeline waited.

"I need to keep a low profile these days because I'm trying to gain custody of my half sister." Cal let go of her, and reached into his pocket. He pulled out his wallet and flipped it open to a worn photo of a grinning preteen with braces. "Of course, she's sixteen and twice as much trouble now."

"She's a half sister?" Madeline couldn't help but be intrigued by this rare glimpse of Cal Turner's private life, even if he had delivered a healthy blow to her ego tonight.

"After my mom left us, my dad married Allison's

mom and Allison was born a couple of years later." Cal traced his thumb over the little girl's smiling face before snapping the leather billfold closed. "We were pretty close, even after I left Tennessee, but when Dad and Allison's mother died in that crash this spring..."

Madeline squeezed his hand, unsure what other comfort to give. "I know that hit you hard."

Cal shrugged. "My dad and I had worked out our differences before then, but I know Allison is still pretty torn up. She stayed with her aunt for a few weeks and then called me to come get her. She moved in with me over the summer, and I'm trying to gain legal custody."

"I bet that's a project." Madeline recalled her father's headaches when he'd made a motion to obtain sole custody of his only daughter. Cal's battle would no doubt be twice as hard.

"Especially when Allison's aunt Delia is convinced I'm a bad influence." Cal shook his head. "The woman has never forgiven me for riding around the neighborhood on a motorcycle when I was a teenager. You know those people who see a motorcycle and right away assume you're a Hell's Angel, ready to spirit away their daughters?"

Madeline had never seen a Hell's Angel or been worried about anyone spiriting her off, but the idea sounded sort of exciting. She nodded, eager to hear the rest of the story.

"Anyway, Aunt Delia is contesting the motion and trying to prevent me from winning guardianship. Not that Delia wants to take care of Allison herself—she just can't bear to see me win this suit."

"What a nightmare." Madeline couldn't have felt like more of a heel for worrying about her problems when Cal's seemed so much bigger. It also deflated her to realize that Cal hadn't considered her a close enough friend to share this part of his personal life.

"And there are other hoops to jump through," Cal continued. "Mostly because Allison's a certifiable genius. She started classes here this semester."

"Here? At U of L?"

Cal grinned, brotherly pride lighting his features. "She graduated high school early and now she's tackling college."

"A sixteen-year-old in college." Madeline shook her head. "You have your hands full."

"I don't know, Maddy. Sometimes I think she's more mature than me."

Madeline knew a thing or two about gifted students, and she doubted that was the case. Highly intelligent people often hid social uncertainty behind a screen of erudite conversation. She didn't share her insights with Cal, though. He had enough on his mind.

"But I wanted you to know what I'm trying to do so you'll understand why I can't take you up on a very tempting offer." He lifted her hands to his lips and graced the back of each one with a chaste kiss. "I've got to mend a reputation that's been a lifetime in the making, so I can't take any chances making a splash on campus now. Especially with you being a grad student."

Madeline nodded and pulled back her hands. She hadn't given much thought to that particular issue. She'd known Cal before he'd even started teaching.

"It's okay. I mean, it would have been great if you could have helped me, but I'll figure something out."

Cal frowned. "What do you mean by that?"

"I mean, I'll come up with another plan to get my dissertation approved." Her mind had already started to brainstorm, searching for a new approach to the problem as she backed toward the door.

He nodded and flashed her a wink. "Okay. Just as long as there are no more steamy propositions involved."

Maybe the wretched happenings of her day had made her less circumspect than usual, but for some reason Madeline couldn't suppress a wicked giggle. "As a purveyor of human mating rituals, steamy propositions are my new business, Cal."

She pushed open the door, wondering why he was scowling. "Don't worry about me. And good luck with your sister!"

As Madeline squeaked down the corridor in her sensible shoes, she tried not to think about how deliciously gratifying a night with Cal Turner would have been. She couldn't very well force the man.

Instead, she focused on the new plan of action quickly taking shape in her head. Since she wouldn't be gaining any notice—or notoriety—on the arm of the campus playboy, it was clearly time for Madeline Watson to invest in a red dress.

As Cal stepped out of his vintage Chevy in the shopping mall parking lot the next day, he didn't take any of his usual pleasure in the compliments strangers tossed his way.

He nodded in acknowledgment of one teen's, "Nice ride, man," but his heart wasn't in it. His day at the new garage had been tormented with thoughts of Madeline. He'd attempted to suppress thoughts of her in the scramble to move into his new office, but no matter how hard he tried, he hadn't been able to excise Maddy or her tempting request from his mind. He'd been awake half the night envisioning just how rewarding it would have been to take the Lady Scholar to his bed.

Not that he regretted his decision, he assured himself as he strode through the mall, peering into one store after another in search of his shopaholic half sister. Really, what choice did he have? Allison's well-being meant more to him than his own. His first priority was to secure guardianship of her and to get her settled in school. He didn't imagine Aunt Delia would send an investigator up from Tennessee to spy on him or anything, but he did worry that the social services department would watch him all the more closely because she was contesting his suit for custody. Who knew when they would track him down for a surprise visit?

Besides, Allison required some stability in her life again, and she needed to cultivate some pleasures besides shopping. That meant Cal needed to spend more time with her. An affair with Maddy, especially a very public affair, was out of the question.

Refusing to think about what man Maddy might approach next with her scheme, Cal concentrated on finding his sister and getting out of shopper's heaven. His mother's main passion in life was shopping, and she had dragged her only son with her day after day to in-dulge her addiction.

Or at least she had until his father's money ran out and she'd moved on to more lucrative husbands. By Cal's calculation, Mom was now on spouse number six, while Cal's shopping aversion remained unchanged.

Allison's voice cut through his brooding. "Over here, Cal!"

He located her in the food court, surrounded by packages and grinning triumphantly. Today, as always, she wore every conceivable gadget on her body—rings, bangles, handbag, scarf, hat, belt, pins. The theme today seemed to be "cowgirl," because she wore a cowboy hat he'd never seen before, Western boots with a denim skirt, and about ten turquoise neck-laces. The purse she carried looked like a saddlebag, complete with a silver sheriff's star pinned to the brown leather strap.

"The Limited was having a sale," she announced, gesturing toward the overflowing bags.

Cal hated to squash her enthusiasm, but she had to ease off the spending. He'd indulged her so far, be-cause he couldn't bear to say no to a grieving child, but he couldn't see hocking his collection of classic cars to support Allison's shopping addiction.

"We'll talk about the mountain of purchases later." He reached for the bags. "I need to get going, though, I—"

At her pout, he noticed her half-eaten bagel and full cup of soda.

"Okay." He pulled out one of the metal chairs and

straddled it, joining her at the small table. "Five minutes, but then I've got to take you home so I can go back to the garage."

"Thanks, Cal." Allison twirled her short blond braid between her fingers and launched into a description of her day, complete with imitations of her professors.

Cal relaxed for the first time since Maddy's proposal, grateful for his sister's ability to remind him of his priorities. Allison was smart, funny and warmhearted, and she deserved every bit of love and security Cal could give her.

The afternoon was improving by the minute until Cal caught sight of the women's lingerie store just outside the food court. Or rather, the afternoon was improving until Cal caught sight of a particular woman *entering* the lingerie store directly behind Allison's Stetson.

He would recognize the signature button-down shirt and slouchy skirt anywhere. Madeline Watson's heavy leather shoes tread silently on the marble floor, allowing her to walk through life without turning any heads but his.

Cal forgot his promise to himself to not think about her. He lost track of Allison's story as he watched Maddy through the clear glass of the store front window.

Her ethereal profile seemed all the more delicate in contrast to the large frames of her tortoiseshell glasses. Her dark hair twirled around her head in a seemingly endless spiral, finally tucking back down inside itself to form a weighty knot.

Cal's fingers itched to touch that silky mass. Would it be as long as he imagined?

His gaze dropped lower, hungry for more of her, when his eyes encountered a sign that sent a flash fire through his veins.

He'd never spied on a woman before, but he couldn't have torn his gaze from the scene in front of him if a vintage Duesenberg rolled down the mall corridor. Less than thirty feet away, Madeline Watson lingered over a display table labeled Bikinis And Thongs.

"Cal, you haven't heard one word I've said, have you?" The concern in Allison's voice drifted through his consciousness.

"Um, yeah," Cal managed to reply, reaching absently for his sister's soda. He took a long swig, but the icy drink failed to cool the heat generated by quiet, unassuming Maddy as she lifted a scrap of black silk and lace from the pile.

Somewhere, in the foggy recesses of his brain, Cal registered the fact that Allison swiveled in her chair to follow his gaze.

"Did the lingerie shop put up new pictures or something?"

Cal couldn't find words to respond because Maddy chose that moment to toss a handful of Bikinis And Thongs into a small shopping basket.

Visions of the Lady Scholar in her glasses and black panties robbed him of breath. Not that he'd ever mentally undressed her before, but if he had, he would have pegged her for white cotton. The addition of black silk to his fantasies would make Madeline all the more difficult to forget.

The cowgirl turned toward him again. "Hey, isn't that Professor Watson?"

The sound of her name brought Cal crashing back to reality. Before he could think of an appropriate answer, Allison was tossing her leftovers into the garbage and gathering her deputized saddlebag.

She gave him an elbow nudge. "Come on, let's go say hi."

Horror crawled through him in the wake of Allison's rustling shopping bags. "Wait, Al. I don't think we should...." He rose to halt his sister, unwilling to confront Maddy while she shopped for sexy lingerie.

Allison merely waved him forward as she pulled open the door to the store. "Come on!" she called airily, strolling inside and missing the thunderous look he purposely threw her way.

Cal followed, silently vowing to wring his sister's neck. Why had he ever encouraged Allison to sign up for Maddy's class at the university?

He hesitated at the door, knowing he had no choice but to say hello, yet cursing his bad luck just the same. Taking a deep breath, he stepped inside.

A feminine, floral scent assailed him. Silk, lace and satin draped the bright pink walls of the store. Some guys might feel comfortable in a feminine domain such as this, but Cal Turner was not one of them. He jammed his hands into his pockets to prevent himself from inadvertently knocking some delicate item from its perch and consoled himself by imagining this was how some women felt when they entered a garage for the first time.

On the other side of a rack of garter belts, he could

hear Allison rambling in sixteen-year-old fashion. "...so when I want to shop after school, Cal picks me up in time for dinner."

He also heard the trepidation in Maddy's voice.

"Cal?"

If there had been a way to retreat, he would have. But his only option was to ditch his sister, and Cal wasn't about to do that, especially not in some racy lingerie store.

Stepping around the rack into the aisle, Cal brazened it out. "Hey, Maddy." He knew Madeline would probably feel twice as awkward as he did. He grabbed his sister's arm and tugged Allison toward the door. "We were just headed home."

All Madeline had to do was toss him a token "Nice to see you," and he would be home free.

"Wait." She hurried toward them, toting her own armfull of shopping bags and the basket containing enough lingerie to fuel a man's dreams for a year. "As long as you're here, would you mind giving me a man's opinion on a little purchase?"

Sweat beaded on his forehead as Maddy set down her basket. He caught another glimpse of its provocative contents and swallowed. Hard.

Before she could reach for anything titillating, Cal nudged his sister in front of him.

"Allison knows more about that stuff than me." Cal knew Maddy wouldn't show anything too suggestive to his sixteen-year-old sister.

Madeline frowned. "But I wanted to see what you—"

"Really, she does. Did I mention she is a certified genius?" He squeezed his sister's shoulders with what he hoped looked like brotherly affection and not a controlled urge to strangle her.

Obviously the time had come to ditch his sister. There was no way Cal could view Madeline's slinky purchases without breaking his vow to live a more circumspect life. With the black silk and yesterday's torrid proposal both working against him, Cal was about ten seconds away from spiriting Madeline out of the store and cashing in on her offer to fire up the sheets.

What else could a guy do besides cut his losses and run? Maybe Maddy would be forced to make more conservative choices with his sister in tow. Although Cal had the feeling that even Maddy in white cotton would have him sinking to his knees singing a hallelujah chorus. He edged closer to the door. "I, uh, parked at the main entrance, Allison, just come on out when you ladies finish up here."

"But—" Madeline took a step toward him.

"See you soon, Maddy," he rushed on, flashing her a forced grin and a wave as he backed out the door.

He pretended to not hear when his sister called to him.

He waited alone in his car for a good half hour before his breathing returned to normal. When Allison finally appeared at the car door, he had no interest in hearing what the two women might have discussed. He flicked on the radio to avoid a conversation that might induce further torturous thoughts.

As he started the car and headed home, Cal was plagued by images of Madeline holding the black panties between her delicate fingertips. The worst part was that Cal knew she wasn't buying that scrap of lace for him.

Apparently, Maddy's plan to gain some mating rituals experience would now target another guy. The lingerie that Cal had spied would be used to seduce someone else. Cal would never have the pleasure of seeing Madeline unbutton her bulky men's shirt to reveal the skinny black straps of a lace bra. That satisfaction would be given to another man. The thought caused his gut to twist.

After his hellish experience today, Cal now had one more reason to hate shopping malls. From now on, Allison would have to find another way home from her favorite haunt, because Cal wasn't venturing anywhere near the sight of black satin for a long time.

3

THE TRANSITION from wallflower to bombshell wasn't going to be easy, but Madeline thought if her eyelashes could only support a few more coats of mascara, she might have a fighting chance.

At very least, her red dress fit the bombshell mode. What would Cal say if he could see her now decked in the sexiest thing she'd ever owned? Would he be so quick to refuse her?

She'd hoped to get his opinion on the dress at the mall, but he'd been too busy running from her to look at it.

Madeline stepped back from the full-length mirror in the women's locker room. The university gym was deserted on Friday nights, making it a perfect place for her transformation. Because she hadn't really wanted to prance around her neighborhood in the raw silk sheath, she'd decided to get ready for her evening out at work. She'd brought her new outfit and a shopping bag full of makeup to school this morning, and she'd spent the past hour attempting to follow all the instructions the woman at the cosmetic counter had given her.

She stared at her image critically, trying to decide if her eyeliner made her eyes look lopsided, when the door to the locker room squeaked.

Thank goodness. Help had arrived.

The cavalry appeared in the form of Dr. Rose Marie Blakely. The six-foot-tall, imposing sociology department chair met Madeline's gaze in the mirror's reflection.

"Holy Toledo, Maddy, what happened to you?" Rose Marie yanked Madeline around to look at her firsthand. "I can't decide if you're going for Oscar Night glamour or the Whore of Babylon look."

Although Rose Marie was twenty years older than Madeline and as uninhibited as Madeline was guarded, the women had formed a solid friendship in Madeline's years at U of L. They frequently ate lunch together and stayed late at the university talking about work.

"The dress is killer," Rose Marie observed, flipping her long blond hair over her shoulder as she nodded approval at the short sheath with tiny rhinestone buckles at the waist. She walked in a precise circle around Madeline, her uncommon height and girth giving her the look of a fabled Amazon warrior. "But despite the makeup, you look like you haven't slept in days."

Hmm. Madeline had rather hoped she looked a step above insomniac. After Cal Turner had turned her down flat, she'd decided she wouldn't waste any more years stuck inside her haphazard dress and hiding behind her glasses. She'd been living in the ivory tower too long, sheltered by the academic world she'd called home since her childhood with her single father the professor. Maybe if her mom had stuck around she might have cultivated more in the feminine wiles department.

Maddy frowned. "Not quite. I called you here because I obviously need some help."

She might not be able to coerce Cal into helping her cultivate a more worldly reputation, but with a little effort, she felt sure she could attract another man's notice.

Although she was finding it difficult to work up much enthusiasm for the project now that her target had to be someone other than Cal. Maybe she should forget about experiencing the mating dance and just observe....

No. She would not chicken out just because Cal rejected her. She would prove to him, and herself, that she could do this.

With her dissertation project all but swinging in the gallows, she had to act fast. She couldn't wait around for Cal to gain guardianship of his sister—if that was even his real reason for not going out with her.

If she didn't start changing her reputation in a hurry, the dissertation committee would nix her mating rituals study for good. Then she'd turn into a crusty old academic, researching something boring like literary sociology because she was an uptight prude with the social skills of a robot.

This dissertation was important to her—a departure from her usual staid research projects. For once, she would have the courage to conduct an investigative study that truly interested her.

Dr. Rose stepped closer and ran her fingers beneath Madeline's eye. She peered down at the black goo left on her fingers. "Good Lord, the dark circles are makeup?"

Madeline shrugged, pointing to the bench with her bagful of cosmetic loot. "The saleswoman suggested one of everything, since I didn't have anything to start with."

Rose Marie raised her finely arched eyebrows. "Oh, did she now?" She stepped over to the bench and peered inside the bag. "Vitamin C serum. Revitalizing concealer cream. Eyebrow gel?" Rose Marie pawed through the contents, shaking her head and sending long hair dancing across her floral blazer. "What exactly did you use?"

"A little of everything."

"Everything?"

"I wouldn't have lugged it all around campus, Rose, if I didn't think I had to use it all."

Rose Marie puffed out a martyred sigh and pointed a manicured nail toward the bathroom. "Okay, Maddy. Dig out your oxidizing facial scrub and wash all that stuff off."

Madeline scooped up her cotton robe and a towel and did as she was bid. One didn't question the wisdom of Dr. Rose.

"And remind me to get you a subscription to *Cosmo* for your birthday," Rose Marie shouted. "I can't believe you've never worn makeup before."

"My father said serious scholars don't wear makeup," Madeline called over the running water. Then, realizing her gaffe as she envisioned Rose Marie's precisely defined red lips, Madeline added, "Of course, he can be a little closed-minded."

By the time Madeline had banished every trace of

her failed makeover, Rose Marie had set up a chair in front of the mirror.

"I'm taking over here, Maddy. Have a seat." Rose Marie burrowed into the cosmetic bag. "But in exchange I want to know exactly what you're up to tonight."

While Rose Marie patted Madeline's face with powder, Madeline kept her story as simple as she could. She omitted her encounter with Cal, of course. There was no sense relating that embarrassing tale.

"So you're going out on the town tonight in pursuit of a man to flaunt around campus...preferably a guy who can't keep his hands off you in public and who can effectively tarnish your reputation."

Madeline squinted to see what Rose Marie did with her little makeup brush. Unfortunately, Madeline could scarcely see beyond her nose without her glasses. "Pretty much."

"Has it occurred to you that maybe you ought to just give the committee time to adjust to the idea of your mating rituals study?" Rose Marie suggested. "Maybe you should wait a few weeks and propose it again."

Madeline shook her head. "I can't risk them turning it down twice. I didn't get involved in sociology so I could study books. I want to study people."

"Personally, I love the concept." Rose Marie flicked a skinny brush across Madeline's eyelid with efficient strokes. "I might be able to help find a more supportive faculty member to sit on your committee, but you know I can't interfere with the committee's eventual decision."

Madeline halted Rose Marie's hand and looked her in the eye. "I would never ask you to."

Nodding, Rose Marie clicked one small compact closed, then opened another. "Okay. But tell me this. Just how are you going to say a graceful good-night to your male prospect tonight when he tries to take you back to his place?"

A little flutter of fear rolled through her. "I hadn't really thought of that." If Cal had accepted her proposal, she wouldn't have to concern herself with fighting off a man. Instead, Cal would be stuck fending off *her* advances.

"The Commonwealth of Kentucky boasts some fine young men, Maddy, but you can't count on every one of them being a gentleman. You need to be careful." Rose Marie reached for the topknot on Madeline's head and unfastened the scrunchy. "Wow! You look like Morticia."

Madeline eyed her damp hair. "It's sort of flat. I usually just leave it up."

"When you called me for help, you were admitting I'm the expert. Now sit still while I find the blow-dryer and we'll give you some serious glam."

Thirty minutes later Madeline walked out of the gym in her red dress and heels, her long hair swinging a seductive rhythm against her back. Sure, she still had her glasses on, but Rose Marie had assured her she was a knock-out.

Besides, she couldn't watch what was happening around her if she couldn't see. How sexy would it be if she accidentally drank from a flower arrangement, mistaking it for a fruity umbrella drink? Madeline promised herself she would think about getting contacts next week.

She felt different with her hair down…more daring, maybe a little decadent. Rose Marie had ended up putting barely any makeup on her, but she'd spent half an hour blow-drying Madeline's long hair and brushing the ends so they would curl under.

Madeline was just about ready to go out, except that she wanted to retrieve the can of Mace she kept in the desk drawer at her office. Ever since one of the teachers had been assaulted by a student, Madeline had kept the can tucked away just in case. After Rose Marie's warning about ardent gentlemen, Madeline decided to take it along for her night on the town.

Certainly her reason for going back to her office didn't have anything to do with the fact that Cal taught a continuing education business class on Friday nights. Or that Madeline would have to walk right by his building.

Okay, maybe a little part of her wished Cal would see her the one time in her life she had ever looked marginally sexy. And it wouldn't hurt to gauge one man's reaction to her appearance before she subjected herself to the larger test of the popular dance club she was planning to hit tonight. Seeing Cal would be like a trial run. A scientific experiment.

Rapidly rationalizing her plan, Maddy slowed outside of Honors Hall and waited for Cal's class to emerge. She paced in front of the stately brick building in the twilight, making sure she remained on the sidewalk so her high heels wouldn't sink into the damp grass.

To distract herself, she thought about how different the University of Louisville looked from Rensselaer Polytechnic Institute, the campus where her father worked which was practically her hometown. Where Rensselaer had been sleek and new, Louisville was traditional and dignified. She loved the mishmash of brick buildings, the flowering trees and the rampant cardinals the school had adopted as its mascot.

The pace was slower here and Madeline appreciated that. Even though she'd worked hard to make a place for herself in the academic world, the environment here wasn't as cutthroat as in her father's realm.

She pushed her glasses up on her nose, belatedly recognizing the telltale sign of nervousness carried over from her youth.

"This is silly," she muttered, annoyed with herself for stalking a guy as if she were a lovelorn teenager.

Despite Cal's playboy reputation, Madeline knew he was a sharp man with a successful business to run and a busy life to manage. He didn't need her and her adolescent schemes taking up his time.

She turned on her heel to leave just as the double doors swung wide and a small troop of students emerged.

Madeline picked up her speed, not an easy task in spike heels. Now that she had talked herself out of her plan, she definitely didn't want to be caught loitering outside Cal's class.

"MADDY?"

Cal watched the woman in the red dress walk away, wondering if he had dreamed the resemblance to Madeline. He squinted to get a better view of her in the growing dusk.

He hardly ever took note of flashy women anymore, having outgrown that particular preference long ago. He'd worn himself out on the insubstantial type in that year of living hell after his divorce.

But something about this woman had grabbed his attention. There was a familiarity to her efficient little walk, her regal bearing, that sent a message of quiet reserve in spite of her sexy get-up.

"Maddy?" he called her name again. If it had been her, wouldn't she have turned around?

He stepped up the pace, determined to satisfy his curiosity. He didn't think it really could be her. After all, what would the Lady Scholar be doing garbed in come-hither shoes and a dress three inches shy of her knees?

And then he knew. It was Friday night, and Madeline Watson was putting her plan into effect.

Searching for a man to seduce.

Oh, God.

Fury kicked through him, sending his legs into a sprint. He caught her in ten strides. One firm tug on her slender arm caused her to topple off her heels and straight into his arms.

"Oh!" Her breathless gasp would have confirmed her identity, even if his gut instinct hadn't.

For one mind-numbing moment Maddy lingered against him, imprinting her compact curves on his body. Lust mingled with the anger simmering in his veins.

She looked gorgeous. Sexy as hell in her tiny silk

dress, she revealed a tantalizing glimpse of skin. She was every inch the temptress, glasses perched on her nose and all. There was something incredibly appealing about a woman in a little red dress who wore glasses.

Her hair swirled around her like a dark sea. The strands shimmered and swayed in the streetlight as she moved, robbing her of her usual reserved look.

He used both hands to steady her.

Or to feel her. He couldn't honestly say which.

But his hands fit right into the notch of her waist as if they were meant to be there. The smooth silk of her dress seemed to beg for his touch, but he contented himself with gently smoothing the fabric over her hips.

"Cal." She straightened and stepped away from him. "You startled me."

He took in the dress and the expanse of long leg it revealed. Her shoulders were bared to his gaze, too, exposing golden skin and thin tan lines from a bathing suit. Looking down at her, he glimpsed a tantalizing hint of cleavage and…good Lord. Was that body glitter she had dusted in that particular curve?

The scent of raspberries seemed to emanate from her and he nearly groaned with the torment. He couldn't have been more aroused if she'd strutted by him naked.

Then again…

"Good night, Mr. Turner!" One of his students waved as he jogged by, forcing Cal to recall where they were.

"See you next week," he returned absently.

"I'd better go, too," Maddy announced, spinning away from him.

"No." He anchored her to him by the arm.

"No? What do you mean, no?" She glared up at him with the same mutinous look Allison had given him when he'd taken away her credit card yesterday.

"I mean, not yet. Not until you tell me what you're doing traipsing around campus alone after dark in a dress like that."

She tilted her chin toward him. "I do *not* traipse."

As another evening class let out around them, Cal heard a low wolf whistle among the crowd. He didn't have to look around him to know the target.

He hustled Madeline toward the parking lot, wishing he had a jacket to toss over her shoulders. "Well, there you have it, gorgeous. You've already collected your first bit of research for your dissertation."

She stumbled along next to him, apparently forgetting to be angry when her intellectual curiosity was piqued. "I have?"

He pressed his advantage and hurried her toward his car while she was distracted. "The wolf whistle is one of the earliest possible steps in a mating process."

"What wolf whistle?" She stopped and peered around her, wide-eyed, as if waiting for wild hounds to emerge from the trees around campus.

"Come on, honey, I'll explain it to you once we get to my car." He couldn't really account for his sudden need to hide her from anyone's eyes but his own. In fact, he wasn't sure he cared to examine his motivation right now. But that didn't stop him from tugging her forward once more.

Madeline withdrew her arm. "Sorry, Cal, but I need to go to my office."

"You were planning to walk all the way to your office and back by yourself after dark?" He searched the campus with his gaze, knowing the kinds of predators that lurked at night, searching for solitary coeds—or foolish teachers.

"I frequently walk around campus after dark," she informed him, rocking back on her tiny heels.

"Not in those shoes you don't. You're dangerous tonight, Maddy."

She grinned. "That's great, Cal. Dangerous is just the look I was going after."

Jealousy seared his insides like a blowtorch. "Why? You got a date with some bad-ass to flaunt at university mixers?"

The Lady Scholar folded her arms across her eye-popping dress and cocked her head to one side. "The bad-ass of my choice wasn't available."

That soothed him somewhat...assuming she referred to him. "Then if you don't have a date, what are you doing dressed to the nines in a piece of silk no bigger than a place mat?"

"I'm on the prowl."

"Over my dead body, maybe."

Her jaw dropped, and for a moment her sassy new attitude gave way to the more conservative woman he'd known the past four years. "Cal Turner, you have no right to gainsay me."

"You're my friend and I have every right to protect you from yourself."

"I'm not doing anything different than the average American single woman does on any given weekend!"

"Honey, that just goes to show you how little you know about this whole process. Women don't go out by themselves. They travel in packs for safety. Yet here you are, all alone and vulnerable as can be."

She brightened. "I won't be vulnerable once I go back to my office."

"What are you hiding in there? A few members of the football team?" Maybe he didn't want to know the answer. Maddy was full of surprises this week.

"My can of Mace."

She was even more hell-bent for trouble than his sister. "Oh, I feel better now, Maddy. That'll help." Unwilling to debate a topic he wasn't going to give an inch on, Cal placed his hands on Madeline's shoulders.

She was normally a good five inches shorter than him, but tonight, in her heels, they were nearer to eye level. Her skin felt cool to the touch and she shivered with her whole body.

Was it the cold? Or had his touch affected her that way? Intrigued, he pulled her a little closer.

She came willingly, gazing up into his eyes as if there was nothing unusual about him brushing greedy fingers over her bare skin in the moonlight.

That fact only proved to him that she was too naive. There was no way he could let her go out alone tonight.

"Frankly, I don't trust the Mace," he continued. "In fact, I don't know that I'd trust the football team with you either. Not when you look like that."

She smiled. "I'll be fine, Cal."

He shared her grin and leaned in closer. The heat between them growled to life like a throaty engine. "I know you will, gorgeous, because I'm going with you."

She started to pull away, but he halted her by sliding his fingertips over the smooth flesh of her upper arms.

Her answering shiver roused and scared him in equal measure. It amazed him that he kept her captive there with no more than his touch. How would he ever endure an evening with a woman who had more fire-power than fuel injection?

"Cal—"

"Meet your date for the night, Maddy." He stroked a lazy finger across her collarbone. "The bad-ass of your choice is officially at your service."

4

THE HEADY SENSATION of Cal's thumb rolling over her shoulder distracted her, but not so much that she missed his words. "Excuse me?"

He pulled her toward the parking lot. "I said I'm coming with you, Maddy. Let's go."

"Wait a minute." She dug her red suede heels into the loose gravel of the small parking lot currently under construction. She would sacrifice the shoes before she let Cal Turner lead her around by the nose. Or by her hormones. "I thought you couldn't risk adding more scandal to your reputation?"

He gestured toward her outfit. "That was before I realized the lengths you would go to for this project of yours. I'm not about to let you risk your neck."

Frustration simmered through her. "Thanks, Cal, but it's *my* neck to risk." She spun on her heel, determined to get to her office and leave him to his newfound morality.

Before she took two steps, she found herself plucked from the ground and cradled in his arms like a new bride about to be carried across the threshold.

"Fine. Risk your neck all you want, but I'm driving." He crossed the gravel lot near the new construction.

"Cal!" the little squeal she made sounded nothing like her. She would be angry at his presumptuousness if she wasn't so deliciously aware of every square inch of her body that he touched.

With one arm wrapped just below her shoulders, and one arm supporting her thighs, Cal wreaked havoc on her senses. His fingers rested on a patch of bare skin beneath the hem of her dress, and although he kept his hand very still, Madeline couldn't help but imagine what it would feel like if he put those fingers in motion.

She'd never suspected a male body could be so hard and unrelenting, sort of like Cal's personality. But those qualities were much more appealing in their physical manifestation than as part of his overall character. Right now, Madeline could hardly string two thoughts together with all that masculine strength surrounding her.

"Put me down!" she snapped.

He grinned, apparently less annoyed than he had been a few minutes ago. "I don't even park my car in this dusty gravel. You think I'd let your sexy little self walk across it in new suede shoes?" He set her down when they reached the other side of the lot.

Disappointment warred with relief when Maddy's toes hit the ground. How was it that he could have her senses singing concertos while he seemed as unaffected as if he'd done no more than change her oil?

He searched his pocket for his keys while she fumed. "I'll only ditch you the first chance I get," she said, folding her arms across her chest.

Finding the keys, he held them up like a prize and winked. "Honey, it won't be easy with me glued to you."

An unwanted shiver trembled over her. The image

of them joined together was too enticing to contemplate. She knew that's not what he meant. Knew that wasn't what he wanted. Still...

He unlocked a car door while she chided herself. She needed to forget about Cal and his noble intentions tonight if she wanted to make any headway into her research. It wouldn't be easy with his gorgeous body at her side, but if she wanted to get serious about changing her reputation, she needed to find a man whose thoughts weren't so pure.

The idea seemed grossly unappealing after experiencing Cal's touch. How could she settle for anyone else's?

"You ready?"

Cal's words beckoned her from her musings and she turned to join him. Only then did she realize what kind of car he'd led them to.

She stared, immobile, her gaze running over the lines of his Chevy. "Ohmigod."

"You don't like it?"

Like it? The car looked almost as good as the man standing next to it.

She took in the dark blue exterior and white top of the classic car. Either the paint had been kept in mint condition or Cal had repainted with the original color, because the car looked as new and authentic as if it had just rolled off the production line. Because her father had been the only family she'd ever known, Madeline had grown up talking cars and physics the way most girls talked about Barbie dolls and boys.

He jingled the keys in his pocket. "It's a—"

"Fifty-seven. It's gorgeous, Cal." Madeline moved

closer, brushing her fingers appreciatively along the white seat, also original. For a moment she wished she had worn saddle shoes and a poodle skirt instead of her red dress. "This is the hot-rod version, I'll bet."

He shrugged, but the little grin playing around his lips told her she had guessed correctly. "You know something about cars?"

She shook her head. "Not enough to change my own oil, obviously." She'd been taking her Honda to Cal or one of his garages ever since she'd arrived in Louisville. "But my dad has a lifetime subscription to *Car and Driver*. I read a little here and there so I could share his interest." She'd never acquired her father's taste for physics, but she had soaked up his enthusiasm for vintage automobiles to have something to talk to him about.

"You must have read more than a little." He nodded toward the car. "Hop in."

Madeline forgot all about her reluctance to go with him. Not only was she eager for her first ride in a '57 Chevy, she also couldn't deny the lure of a chance to learn more about Cal. She'd bet her tenure slot this vehicle meant more to him than his successful chain of car repair shops. Why hadn't she known that about him before?

After she took her seat, Cal closed the door behind her and went around to the driver's side.

"Where to?" he asked, switching on the ignition. "I'm at your disposal tonight, Maddy. Use me as you wish."

To cover her nervousness, she adjusted her glasses, a habit she'd been trying to break since adolescence.

"Since we both know you're only willing to go so far—"

"You know, I can't wait to see if you're still dangling that offer in front of me in two weeks after the custody hearing is all over." His gaze held hers across the car interior, promising sweet retribution for her teasing. "Hasn't anybody ever taught you to not play with fire?"

She shifted in her seat. "Obviously that's a lesson I've practiced *too* well up until now, Cal. When even the university administration thinks I'm too much of a prude to research sex, it's time to start letting myself get burned."

He wiped a weary hand across his face and groaned. "What am I going to do with you, Maddy?"

"You can squire me around town tonight, if you want." He hadn't really left her much choice.

"No offense, gorgeous, but I'm trying to salvage my reputation, not add to it. I'm not about to give the social services department or Auntie Delia any chance to deny my guardianship."

"But it's not like we're going to a strip bar or anything. And I'm not going to do anything outrageous." She wouldn't want Cal to jeopardize custody of Allison.

Slowly, Cal nodded. "We'll go someplace tame?"

"I was thinking Coyotes might be a good place for my first foray into the mating scene."

"A cowboy bar? The two-stepping set will be all over you before we get to the bar. I can't take you there."

"I thought cowboys were notorious for their gentlemanly conduct?"

Cal closed his eyes for a long minute, willing himself to get a grip. Coyotes was a reputable club, so it wasn't as though he'd be risking custody of Allison by accompanying Maddy there for a few hours.

The dark-haired siren across from him was determined to get her way, so he would be wise to just keep his mouth shut and make sure she didn't get into too much trouble.

He only hoped he could keep *himself* out of trouble. How would he go all evening without touching her and tempting himself again? He didn't know what possessed him to tease Maddy with the idea of seducing her after the custody hearing had safely passed. Even after he proved to the social services department that Delia Heywood's complaints about him were unfounded, he wouldn't allow himself to get tangled up with Maddy.

Their worlds would never mesh, and he sure as hell wouldn't subject Allison to an unstable household with his ill-fated relationships.

He just had to keep that in mind when temptation got too strong.

Finally he nodded. "I'll take you there, Maddy, but promise me one thing."

She blinked up at him, her big brown eyes full of an innocence completely at odds with her seductive clothing.

"If anyone asks, you're my date for the night. You got it?"

"What about my quest for a man?"

He couldn't help but grin. "I'm it for tonight, babe."

"But you won't help me convince the administration that I'm a woman of experience." She wrinkled her nose, shifting her glasses on her face. "I need someone to work with me on that."

He shook his head. "There will be no prowling tonight."

She sighed a long-suffering huff that ended in mumbled concord. "Agreed."

Cal slid the car into reverse and took a route through the city. After a quick call to check on his sister at the house, he relaxed into his escort role.

The scent of raspberries tickled his nose and beguiled his senses. When he caught himself wondering if Madeline would taste as good as she smelled, Cal knew he had to distract himself before he pulled over and kissed her senseless, or worse—turned the car around and took her back to her house.

Cal tapped out a rhythm on the steering wheel and tried to think of all the reasons he'd be an idiot to act on his attraction to Maddy. Custody of his sister aside, Cal's poor track record with relationships kept him from showing Madeline all the nuances of seduction. Sure, he'd dated more than his share of women since his move to Louisville, but none of them had threatened his peace of mind the way Maddy did.

He'd been drawn to her the moment they'd met, but he'd only flirted with her because he'd known she'd never take him up on his outrageous proposals. She'd always been a little distant, even once they'd developed a friendship.

And that suited him just fine.

He knew himself too well, knew he would only hurt her if he gave in to the urge to make their relationship more than friendly. Despite the degree on his wall, he was a blue-collar mechanic at heart. His weekends would forever be spent in the garage, not the art gallery.

Madeline might think she would be satisfied with a fling, but he knew her better than that.

"So you're my date?" Madeline asked, fidgeting with the hem of her skirt as he pulled into the parking lot of the city's most glitzy honky-tonk.

Cal had called it a cowboy bar in an effort to dissuade Maddy from going. Knowing full well that the sprawling club was more like a Westernized disco, he pulled up in front of the neon sign featuring a cowboy hat and a pair of feminine legs in bright red heels. No wonder Maddy had wanted to come here, he mused silently. Tonight she epitomized the poster child for footloose females.

He parked the car and hopped out, then opened Maddy's door. Strains of a country-rock combination of music drifted from the bar, along with raucous laughter and shouts.

"I'm your date," Cal repeated, determined she would stick by his side on her fact-gathering mission. "But you're here to work, right?"

He tried to not stare at her legs as she stepped from the car. In the reflected neon light of the flashing marquee, he caught another flash of glitter painted over her breasts when he helped her up. Was it his imagination, or was there a trace of raspberries lingering in the air, too?

He had to be the town's biggest moron to have accompanied her here as her personal bodyguard when what he really wanted to do was take her home, top her with whip cream and steal a taste of her berry-scented body.

"I'm working, but I'm here to have fun, too." She fluffed her hair and did a little shimmy that straightened her dress in some way.

Cal's mouth went dry.

"I mean, that's okay with you, right?" She smiled tentatively, revealing a touch of uncertainty. "We can have a little fun, as long as we don't draw too much attention to ourselves, can't we?"

He found himself nodding, unwilling to disappoint her when she'd obviously worked hard to achieve her ends tonight. He needed to remember she wasn't as at home in her slinky dress and shoes as she appeared. Madeline Watson had probably never donned a pair of high heels before tonight.

As for the body glitter, he'd give his torque wrench to know whether or not she'd been secretly shimmering beneath her bulky men's shirts all these years.

"We can have fun within reason." He found himself draping her long hair over her shoulders in an attempt to cover as much of her bared flesh as possible. "Don't let that red dress go to your head, Maddy."

His fingers toyed with the silky strands, ignoring his brain's command to release them. The music pounding its way out of the club changed to a softer tune, the kind that made line dancers yield the floor to two-steppers.

She peered up at him through her tortoiseshell

glasses, the neon light mirrored across their surface. Cal didn't dare remove them, much as he wanted to. Her teacher-style spectacles helped remind him of who she really was, the kind of woman a man like Cal didn't deserve.

"I wish it would," she whispered across the small space that separated them.

"Hmm?" He'd lost the thread of their conversation somewhere between dreaming of body glitter and lecturing himself on the importance of eyeglasses.

"I wish the red dress would go to my head," Maddy repeated, hugging herself in the cool night air. "Then maybe I wouldn't have to work so hard at this." She flicked the hem of her dress with her fingers. "It's not really me."

Damn. Just now, he wished she was a red dress sort of woman. The kind of red-dress women he usually dated wanted to say goodbye afterward as much as he did. He'd never be able to do that with Maddy.

"It looks like you," he found himself saying. "You'd never know your alter ego wore sensible shoes and graded term papers for fun."

His fingers brushed through her hair, to her cool skin underneath. He curved his palm around the back of her neck, ignoring the niggling voice that reminded him he had no business touching her.

"Really?" She shivered, leaving him no choice but to pull her closer.

"Really." He told himself he was only going to kiss her to give her confidence, to let her know she was as desirable as any woman he'd ever seen.

But, as he leaned in closer, nearing the heady heaven of her soft lips, he knew himself to be a liar.

He was going to kiss her because he wanted to.

"Cal." She breathed his name in the second before his mouth met hers.

She tasted hotter than bourbon on a cold night, and she fired his senses twice as fast. Five years' worth of suppressed desire ignited at one brush of her lips, one delicious stroke of her tongue.

He felt like an engine that had been idling for too long, suddenly revving faster—more erratically—than it should, eager to flex its muscle and test its own power.

Maddy stepped closer, situating herself between his thighs, lightly skimming her body against his. He tensed, debated the wisdom of holding her for all of two seconds, and then enfolded her in his arms.

His hands found her waist and secured her to him, clenching silk-covered curves. He held her there, drinking in the taste of her, wishing they were somewhere where he could search out the source of the raspberry scent that still teased his nose.

If he had the chance to get her alone, he'd never be stupid enough to turn her down again. If he had an hour—no, make that a night—with her, he'd make her forget her hare-brained scheme to hone her seduction skills on a stranger.

Urging her closer, he relished the press of her breasts against his chest, the slide of her silken dress across his clothes.

The sound of another set of high heels clicking on the paved parking lot jarred him. He pulled away from

Maddy, disoriented, just in time to see a jeans-clad couple walk by on the way to their car.

As their footsteps faded, Cal willed his breathing back to normal. He braved a look at Maddy and immediately wished he hadn't. Her steamy glasses tugged at his conscience.

"My God." Of all the stupid things he'd done, this one topped the charts. What if someone had seen them? What if rumors of him out on the town, acting as irresponsibly as a teenager on his first date, reached the social services department? They'd reject his request for guardianship of Allison long before he got the chance to explain.

"Sorry." Madeline touched her lips hesitantly, as if they might have changed since his kiss.

The simple gesture made him want to kiss her all over again. And that kind of thinking could only get him in trouble.

He grabbed her by the hand and pulled her toward the club. "See? The red dress is definitely working." He couldn't hide the growl in his voice. He hadn't been so sexually frustrated since high school.

Maddy, however, sounded pleased. "I guess you're right." She tripped along behind him. "Slow down, Cal. Dr. Rose said a woman needs to make an entrance."

"Dr. Rose?" He curbed his pace, not to help her with her entrance, but only because he didn't want her to twist an ankle. "Don't tell me the queen of male-bashers has been giving you pointers in the manhunt."

"She's very knowledgeable about that sort of thing," Maddy assured him. "I think she's dated a lot."

"Dated and discarded, you mean. She's gone out with half the professors on campus." Rose Marie Blakely had a reputation almost as bad as his. Fleetingly, Cal wondered if Dr. Rose was avoiding a real relationship, too.

"And I'll just bet no one has ever told her she doesn't have enough experience to handle her field of research," Maddy returned. "Maybe they only call her a male-basher because she doesn't let the administration walk all over her."

Cal shrugged, willing to let the subject drop now that they had closed in on their destination.

As they passed through the front doors to the bar, Cal noticed several men pause to look at Maddy. He put his arm around her to reel her in a little closer and then paid the cover charge.

"I'll pay you back," Maddy whispered. "My money's not in a place where I can get to it in public."

Did the woman live to torture him? He had a vision of himself scouting the terrain of her body in search of hidden dollar bills. "This one's on me."

"But—"

"I mean it, Maddy." He couldn't bear any more of Maddy's surprises tonight. They'd only just stepped through the doors, yet he felt as if he'd already been through the wringer.

Music engulfed them. Another pop country tune boomed from the stereo system, giving a rhythm for the dancers and a back beat for the would-be Casanovas as they scoured the room for likely prey. Stetson hats and cowboy boots abounded, but so did khakis and polo shirts. A neon moon hung above a dance floor bigger than the average high school gymnasium.

Cal gripped Maddy's hand, determined she wouldn't stray too far from him. He gritted his teeth at the male attention she garnered, but led her to the bar like a polite date and offered to buy her a drink.

He'd get through this night somehow.

While she waited for her tequila sunrise—a cocktail that suited her dress, according to Maddy—Cal scanned the room. He made meaningful eye contact with a few guys ogling Maddy, effectively communicating her off-limits status.

He guided her to a table, thinking maybe he could do this after all. Another hour or two and he'd convince Maddy to go home. Maybe by then she'd realize that going out on the town wasn't all that exciting.

He'd almost reached a quiet corner when a couple of friends who owned a rival car repair shop stepped out of the crowd to greet Cal. One of the men offered Cal a hearty handshake and a drunken slap on the back.

In the moment that Cal was forced to let go of Maddy, he heard her murmur something about finding some paper for her notes.

Notes?

He swiveled around to grab her, almost knocking over his tipsy friend.

But she was gone.

The red dress had vanished into a sea of womanizing cowboys, leaving nothing but a whiff of raspberries and a trail of turning heads in its wake.

5

FREEDOM.

Madeline savored its sweetness as she hurried away from Cal and his iron grip around her wrist. At least, she tried to convince herself she was savoring her freedom. A little voice in the back of her mind wondered if she wasn't just running away from the wealth of emotions his kiss had fostered tonight.

And what a kiss it had been.

If Cal hadn't pulled away when he had, who knows how far she would have wandered into dangerous territory. She'd temporarily lost all ability to process any sensory impressions outside of him. In other words, she'd been completely, utterly lost in his kiss.

Which probably meant she was as naive about human mating as her dissertation committee seemed to think. She needed to cultivate a little more sophistication about male-female associations before she did something stupid, such as getting caught up in a relationship her work left no time for. Or worse, what if she landed in a relationship and wrought as much heartache as her work-obsessed father had visited upon his lonely wife?

So, despite the tingling in her lips left over from Cal's kiss—or maybe because of it—Madeline told herself she was only too glad to escape him. She might have accepted him as her date for the night, but that didn't mean she had to chain herself to his side, did it?

Tempting as Cal and his spectacle-fogging kisses might be, she refused to forsake tonight's main objective—to observe the basics of human mating rituals.

Cal had made it clear he wouldn't be able to show her the intricacies of flirtation and seduction. Therefore she would focus on learning whatever she could from other men and women in the bar tonight. If she paid close attention, she might begin to see the behavior patterns and learn what techniques were most successful in luring a partner.

The raw data would be similar, on a small scale, to what she would gather for her dissertation. But this information would be used for personal purposes only. Madeline really needed it if she wanted to snag a male to flaunt around campus soon.

This project taunted her, egging her on to succeed in spite of the obstacles. It marked the first topic she'd ever chosen without a care for how it would be professionally received. She'd chosen mating rituals because the subject attracted her, enticed her. She wouldn't back down now, not when she'd spent her whole life succeeding for success's sake.

Her dissertation would be for her sake.

Scoping the massive club for likely sources of paper, Madeline wound her way through the crowd toward the phone booths in the back. Surely she would find a scratch pad of some sort there.

She walked slowly, concentrating on every step in her skyscraper heels so she wouldn't fall. One benefit to walking with Cal had been his solid strength at her fingertips. He balanced her when she teetered.

Somewhere between the dance floor and the phone booths, a crazy man dressed in skintight denim accosted her.

"Hey, hot thing, want to light my fire?" He drifted too close to her unsteady feet, reeking of alcohol. He didn't even bother to look her in the eye, choosing instead to stare straight down her dress.

Madeline resisted the urge to cover her chest with a cocktail napkin. "Looks like you're already lit, cowboy."

She sidled by him without too much trouble since he was falling-down soused anyway. Congratulating herself on routing disaster without the help of her jailer/date, Madeline jumped when a masculine hand wrapped around her forearm.

A new crazy man stood in her path, this one clear-eyed and more intimidating than the drunk. He wore his perfectly combed hair slicked back. His designer silk shirt and Italian-looking shoes probably cost more than Madeline's entire wardrobe. And his cologne almost knocked her over. "Want to dance?"

"No, thank you." She tugged against his grip, but he didn't release her right away.

He pulled her toward the dance floor. "Come on. We'll make your boyfriend jealous."

Unwilling to run back to Cal just yet, Madeline stepped closer to the cologne-doused Don Juan and carefully tread one red suede heel over his toe.

Romeo let her go, but as she hurried away, he called

her a name she'd never been labeled before. At least not within her hearing.

No wonder women traveled in packs. This was insane. Her short walk through the club reminded her of trips down a carnival midway with the hustlers shouting out anything and everything to make her come play their games.

She'd started out ready to have fun, but suddenly she didn't feel like playing anymore.

The phone booths didn't have any paper, so Madeline approached a small bar in the back of the room. After her third unsuccessful attempt to capture the lady bartender's attention, a man at the bar pulled out a stool for her.

"She'll notice you sooner if you have a seat," offered the man, who looked neither dangerous nor drunk. He wore a white button-down shirt similar to the kind Madeline normally wore to school. With his blond hair and blue eyes, he could have just stepped out of a Ralph Lauren advertisement.

In fact, Madeline probably would have thought him handsome if she didn't have Cal on her mind. "Thanks."

She accepted the chair, more for the sake of her sore feet than any haste to accomplish her mission. She didn't know if she was ready to face the crowd again.

The man beside her withdrew his wallet. Madeline watched him reach for a ten-dollar bill.

"You want me to order for you?" the man asked, startling her from her bout of nosiness.

"No thanks," she returned, embarrassed to be

caught staring. "I just needed a pen and paper any-way."

Mr. All-America pulled a ballpoint from his breast pocket and passed it to her along with a cocktail nap-kin. "Here."

She passed it back to him. "Thanks, but I need a little more room to write."

"You can fit at least twenty phone numbers on here." He set the pen and napkin on the bar in front of her. "How much more room could one woman need?"

"I'm taking notes, actually."

He shook his head. "The women are taking notes these days?"

He looked so woeful, Madeline had to laugh.

"No. I'm collecting some data on the singles scene for a paper I'm writing." She thought it sounded better than, *I'm taking notes on the art of seduction so I can lure a man.*

Her companion signaled the barkeeper and ordered a drink for himself along with some paper for her. "You have to admit, that sounds like a pickup line."

"It does?" Fascinated, Madeline scribbled it down on a fresh cocktail napkin for future reference. Why couldn't Cal help her out like this? If he wasn't so busy clamping her to his side like a well-trained dog, maybe he could have given her a few pointers about this sort of thing.

The Ralph Lauren man laughed. "Definitely. If I said that to a woman in here, she'd probably roll her eyes and walk away."

"I don't know." Considering his statement, Made-line lifted the ballpoint to chew on the end, then remembered it wasn't one of hers. "I've heard a lot worse lines in the fifteen minutes I've been here."

The bartender returned with his drink and Madeline's paper. She transferred her one note to the small pad with the club logo blazoned across the top.

"Would you care to hear my spin on the pickup line?" Mr. All-America asked.

Madeline poised her pen for her second notation. "Yes, please."

Grinning, he lightly withdrew the pen from her grasp. "I think I'd like to pitch to the woman and not the researcher, if I may."

Madeline froze. Had she understood this handsome, normal man correctly? He wanted to pick her up?

To buy her a moment's time, she took her first sip of the tequila sunrise she'd ordered with Cal. The concoction singed her throat, but the stinging sensation gave her a moment of much-needed clarity.

She didn't want this.

No matter that she needed a man to help prove to the academic world she was no prude. No matter that she needed experience with seduction—her research topic of choice. What she really *wanted* was Cal.

She smiled back at this nice, normal guy who wasn't for her. "I, um... I'm with a date."

CAL HAD PREPARED HIMSELF to find Madeline bumming a sheet of paper off the doorman or fending off the unwanted advances of some drunken lecher staring down her little red dress.

He would have never guessed that he'd find her cozied up at the bar with what he supposed was a decent-enough-looking guy who wasn't staring down her dress but into her eyes.

Damn.

Cal definitely hadn't prepared himself for the stab of jealousy the Lady Scholar inspired by straightening her glasses in front of another man. Cal had thought *he* was the only one who could fluster her enough to elicit that particular gesture.

So he did what any normal, unprepared man would do when confronted with his own jealousy.

He barreled over to the bar and inserted himself between Maddy and the man who was about to lose a few teeth if he wasn't careful.

Cal smiled, baring enough of his own teeth at the interloper to make his point. "Sorry to break up your play, man, but I sure as hell hope you weren't hitting on my woman just now."

Maddy laid her hand on Cal's back, her touch calming him more than any words she might have offered. "Cal—"

The guy at the bar stood, scraping his chair across the wooden floor. "I take it you're the date." He gathered up his jacket.

"That would be me." Cal folded his arms over his chest, staking his territory. Maybe the guy could keep his teeth as long as he was retreating. Wise move.

"Good luck with your research, miss," he called to Maddy as he backed away. To Cal, he raised a placating hand in the surrender position. "She's all yours, buddy."

Cal nodded, satisfied. Men understood one another. He waited until the man disappeared into the crowd before turning back to Maddy. It was the women who couldn't seem to understand the rules.

He snatched Maddy's notepad off the bar. "You and your research need to come with me."

He offered his hand to assist her, but she remained seated, glaring up at him as if he were the devil's own son. This was not going well.

"Let's get out of here, Maddy, before you get into any more trouble."

She rose to her feet and snatched her notepad back before he realized what she was doing. "You can just go ahead and leave by yourself, Cal Turner. I have no intention of going until I get what I came here for."

That made his blood boil. He leaned closer to her, wanting to make damn sure she heard him over the blare of the music. "Get it through your head, woman, you are not taking a man home with you tonight!"

She lifted her chin and tossed a few feet of hair over one shoulder. "Maybe not, but I can damn well take notes to figure out how to bring one home with me the next time!" She waggled her notepad in front of his nose for emphasis.

Oh, she was going too far. Cal ripped the pad out of her hand and threw it on the bar. "Who needs notes when you're wearing the siren dress? You could walk out of here with any man you choose."

For a moment she looked mad enough to spit bullets. Cal waited for the impact, in fact, knowing he might have gone a little too far by tampering with her notes.

She straightened her glasses and tucked a strand of brown hair behind her ear, making him feel like the world's biggest heel. "I don't think so, Cal. It seems I'm not going to walk out of here with the one I want."

She pivoted on her suede stiletto heels and walked away, using his ten seconds of shock to escape him once again.

Damn.

Had she really wanted to go home with Mr. Apple Pie? Or had she meant someone else?

Either way, he'd acted like a jerk. She hadn't wanted to come here with him tonight, but he'd talked her into it because he couldn't bear to see her get hurt.

Yet, Madeline Watson was obviously a more resourceful woman than he'd given her credit for. Not only had she conquered walking in high heels in the course of an evening, but she had warded off sleazeballs and fended for herself just fine without him.

Knowing he had some apologizing to do, Cal retrieved Maddy's crumpled pad of notepaper from the bar and smoothed the sheets. He added a few more bills to the bartender's jar to make up for the commotion he'd created and the customer he'd run off.

Apparently his bad reputation remained alive and well. Try as he might to keep a clean slate, Cal seemed to have a penchant for making trouble and causing a scene.

He had mishandled this whole week with Maddy. She didn't deserve his jealousy and bad temper when he hadn't even tried to give her the help she needed for her dissertation. He hadn't really considered taking her up on her seductive offer because he knew he'd never be able to have a no-strings relationship with someone like her.

For her sake, maybe he could try. Maybe as long as he started behaving himself in public, he could afford a little misbehavior behind closed doors.

But he would keep that knowledge to himself until he figured out just who Madeline had hoped to go home with tonight.

Edging his way through the crowd, Cal searched for Maddy, a new resolve—and more than a little libido—fueling his steps.

VARIATIONS ON THE LINE "Your place or mine?" ran rampant outside Coyotes. Madeline copied down the words she heard as couples left the bar, smiling to herself at the common theme.

The night air blew cold over her bare shoulders, but she hardly noticed with her indignation to keep her warm. She had taken a seat behind the doorman, safe in the man's burly shadow, but close enough to the exiting couples to observe mating rituals in action.

Her half-hearted research provided some distraction, but mostly she thought about the big scene she'd had with Cal. What had happened to her easygoing friend of two weeks ago? He'd turned from mild-mannered mechanic to uptight chaperone ever since she'd propositioned him. And that was the last thing she needed.

Instead of helping her reach her goal to turn around her reputation, Cal seemed to be trying his best to thwart her efforts.

If she'd had any sense, she would have flirted with Mr. All-America to see what could happen with a man who didn't smother her with protectiveness. But, of course, she didn't have any sense because she had been smitten with Cal for four years and counting.

She blew a big bubble with the piece of gum the doorman had given her and then snapped it with her tongue. Bubble gum was a hidden pleasure—a habit she'd indulged in often since moving out of her father's house. The professor despised gum chewing of any kind.

Madeline looked up when the bar doors swung open again, ready to watch the next couple either say their good-nights or decide who would go with whom.

But the newcomer wasn't part of a lip-locked couple. Cal Turner stood framed in the doorway, his broad shoulders silhouetted in the dim light from the bar.

She said nothing, even when his gaze finally landed on her, hidden behind the doorman. She blew another bubble and then sucked it back into her mouth with a satisfying pop.

"Maddy." He said her name with a warmth that had been absent last time they'd talked. He looked calm now, his hazel eyes relaxed and intent upon her. "I've been looking for you."

He stepped toward her with slow deliberation, the lazy confidence of his stride making her feel a little off balance.

"You found me." She crossed her legs and shifted her notes in her lap, unwilling to pay him any mind.

By some unspoken male agreement, the traitorous doorman vacated his seat and took a walk along the front of the building. Cal pulled the empty folding chair next to Maddy and sat beside her.

"So I did."

She tried to concentrate on her notes, but the words on the paper in front of her didn't exactly take her mind off Cal.

Want to come back to my place?

The line belonged to the most recently departed couple, but Maddy couldn't help but wish it was the kind of thing Cal would say to her.

He withdrew something from his pocket. "I wanted to bring you your paper." He laid her crumpled notes from inside the bar across her lap.

She smoothed the sheets with her hand, thinking maybe she could forgive him. "Thanks."

"And I wanted to apologize."

That caught her attention. She forgot all about the paper and stared into his eyes.

He tilted her chin with the cradle of his hand. "I'm sorry about tonight."

Mesmerized by his tender regard, his gentle touch, Madeline wished she knew what to say to make that small caress last. "It's okay."

He shook his head. "I had no right to embarrass you like that." He paused. "Did you like that guy you were talking to?"

She wanted to close her eyes and burrow deeper into his touch like a contented cat, but she made an effort to focus on Cal's words. "What guy?"

Cal laughed, making the whole world seem right. He rose to his feet and pulled her up beside him. "Come on, I'm taking you home."

She blinked, wondering if he really meant it. "With you?"

He rolled the palms of his hands over her shoulders,

producing a chain of sensual shivers down her spine. "Not tonight."

The heat of his touch held her so spellbound, she almost didn't hear his words. When they registered, the sting of disappointment caused her to pull away.

He pulled her right back to him. "But soon," he whispered. "Come on." He tugged on her arm and started toward the car. "Unless you want me to carry you?"

She started walking. "You can't afford to make a big public scene," she reminded him, even though he'd seemed to enjoy causing them with her tonight. Had he really meant he would take her home one day soon?

"Hop in."

She slid into the car, slipping off her shoes with a sigh of relief. They said little on the short drive to her house, but the quiet comforted her after the sensory overload of the bar.

Cal pulled into her driveway and walked her to the door of her simple two-bedroom ranch house. She felt more shy with him here, on her own front doorstep, than she had all evening.

They stood in darkness since she'd forgotten to leave the light on. A half moon and a faraway street lamp allowed her to see him. Tossing her shoes onto the front porch swing, she wondered what to say.

"Thanks for coming along willingly," Cal said.

She couldn't imagine what accounted for his change of mood since he had railed at her in the bar, but she wasn't about to complain.

"I don't mind following you when you're being reasonable." In fact, she rather liked it. She never tired of the back view of Cal.

He flashed her a slow, lazy smile as he stalked closer. "Then you're going to like what I've got in store for you."

She found herself backed up against the door. Cal leaned against the wooden frame, bracketing her with his arms.

"Is it reasonable?" The cool aluminum of the screened door grazed her thighs on one side, the heat of Cal loomed on the other.

"It's so logical, even you will approve."

Maddy straightened her glasses, wondering if he might do anything to fog them over again. She definitely hoped so. "I'm listening."

"It seems to me that you're looking for two things to help you get your dissertation approved." He took up all her vision, blocking her view of anything but him.

"Two things?" She found it difficult to concentrate, especially since her dissertation was the last thing on her mind at this particular moment.

"You need to change your reputation, which I can't help you with."

She clutched her notes more tightly to her chest, hating the surge of disappointment his words evoked. "Right. Because of your sister's custody hearing."

"But you also genuinely want to acquire some experience in the art of seduction, so you'll feel more acclimated when you start to compile your research."

"I do?"

He brushed his lips over her bare shoulder, igniting

a chain reaction of tingling flesh that tripped all the way to her toes.

And then the implication of his words hit home, bringing with it a dawning delight. "Oh, I do. I need love lessons."

When he stiffened, Madeline feared she'd misinterpreted his meaning. Didn't he want this as much as she did?

Their eyes met, held.

And slowly, Cal nodded. "You're going to need some experience if you're going to become a mating ritual expert."

For a moment his hazel gaze lost the sparkle of humor. The teasing edge he'd adopted since he'd exited the bar vanished. His intent stare pierced her, frightened her, thrilled her.

She could barely squeeze a word past her throat. "Yes."

"And I have an idea where you can procure that experience, Maddy."

She prayed she did, too. She definitely liked the idea Cal's proximity brought to mind.

Her eyes drifted closed just before his lips met hers.

But this was no exploratory kiss like the one he'd given her before they'd entered the bar. This was a culmination of a week of denial—all fire and heat.

She opened to him, eager for the lessons he'd offered, more needy for him now than she had been in four years of secret longing.

He touched her with no part of his body save his lips, yet the coupling of their mouths was a hungry mating in itself, a fevered acknowledgment of the joining they both wanted.

At the moment she could stand no more, when she thought she would die if he didn't touch her, he pulled away.

His chest rose and fell as if he'd run a sprint. His eyes glittered with a predatory gleam that promised fulfillment of their bargain.

"What was that for?" She ran an idle finger over her lips, surprised they didn't feel hot to the touch. She couldn't shake the sensation that he'd left a mark upon her in some way.

He intercepted her hand and brought it to his own lips. "Consider it a first date kiss, Maddy." He kissed her palm and then released it. "I think you're ready for your first lesson in the rules of courtship."

"'Courtship'?" Her brain seemed to backfire when he kissed her like that.

He grinned. "Some people like to engage in a courtship before the actual mating. It's definitely part of the rituals you want to study."

"And you're willing to…teach me?"

"Hands-on lessons, Maddy. Just for you." He backed down her step. "You'll be my one and only student."

6

SCREENED DOOR SLAMMING behind him, Cal padded across his kitchen floor an hour after dropping off Madeline. He'd taken the winding back roads along the Ohio River, hoping to clear his head as he made his way home to the sprawling farmhouse just outside of town. No such luck.

No matter how many times he'd rolled down the window to let the scent of autumn leaves and swampy river wash over him, tension still clamped his temples in a death grip.

Even though he wanted the Lady Scholar more than ever, he wondered if he was just a selfish bastard for cajoling his way into her bed. Had he made a mistake by offering to tutor her in the fine art of seduction?

Tossing his car keys on the table, he told himself a real relationship between them was out of the question. Cal had no desire to marry again, not after the disaster of his first marriage. Katie had soured him on matrimony, had proven to him in no uncertain terms that love didn't transcend social class.

Sure, he was moving up in the world. But he'd never shake his roots.

His lifestyle suited him just fine, but he couldn't imagine the Lady Scholar would like his riverside house on stilts. Too plebeian for her. Maddy lived among the artsy academic types, and would one day graduate to a fancy house amid the rest of Louisville's professorial elite.

She would never see the appeal of Cal's car collection housed in the converted barn and two garages at the side of his property. She might acknowledge the beauty of a classic Chevy, but women never seemed to appreciate the aesthetics of garages.

Cal switched on the light over the kitchen stove and vowed to quit thinking about her. It was bad enough she'd show up in his dreams the moment he closed his eyes. He couldn't torture himself by thinking about her every waking moment, too.

And he definitely wasn't thinking about the black lace panties she'd chosen at the lingerie store.

Reaching for the beer he'd denied himself at the bar, Cal caught a hint of movement in the living room from the reflected light of the refrigerator.

"Allison?"

A sniffle was his only answer.

He slammed the fridge and left the beer on the table, closing the distance between the living room and kitchen in a few strides. "Al? You okay?"

Trying not to worry, Cal flipped on the living room light and spotted his sister huddled on one end of the couch. Tears streaked her face, and she dabbed at her eyes with a wad of tissue. His black lab, Duchess, stood guard beside her.

"Honey, what's wrong?"

He took in the makeup on her face—more than usual—and the floral dress with perfectly matched handbag in her lap.

Didn't Allison usually walk around the house in jeans and a T-shirt?

He encircled her in his arms, and she fell against him, sobbing. Duchess lay at his feet and sighed as if she was glad to be relieved of guard duty.

That's when the key ring fell to the floor.

"I'm so sorry, Cal!"

Cal reached for the keys, thinking he must have caught her red-handed, sneaking back into the house after spending the evening with her friends.

"It's okay hon—" Then he noticed his Thunderbird emblem on the key ring. They weren't house keys, but car keys. His car keys.

Duchess glanced up at him, sensing something was wrong.

"It's just a little dent, Cal, and I didn't mean to—"

Cal tried to quell the panic as he inspected every inch of his baby sister and didn't find a mark. He sank into the sofa, thanking God Allison had arrived home safely.

Then it hit him.

"You took my..." He almost couldn't bear to ask and have his fears confirmed. "You took the Thunder-bird?"

Allison wiped her tears and nodded.

Cal wanted to fall on the floor and cry, too, but he thought it might be more important to console Allison. She looked scared to death.

"You're not hurt?"

She shook her head, covering her mouth to quiet her own crying. Without much success.

"And you didn't hurt anybody else, right?"

Again, she shook her head, making her dangling daisy earrings jingle.

He squeezed her shoulders and willed the words from his mouth. "It's only a car, honey."

Shock seemed to dry the tears. Allison grew still, lifting her head from his shoulder to stare up at him. "Do you mean it?"

Duchess wagged her tail.

"Of course I mean it." He wiped a tear from her cheek, smearing the makeup she rarely wore. "Don't get me wrong, you're still in trouble." He offered her a brotherly grin to lessen the sting of his words. "But not because you hurt the T-bird. You're in trouble for breaking the house rules and putting yourself in a dangerous situation. Not to mention the havoc this could have wreaked on my suit for guardianship."

Allison nodded, wiping the tears from her cheeks with the back of one hand.

"You realize the hearing is just two weeks away, don't you? Why don't we say no more mall visits or anything else after school until then, Al. I think that's an appropriate penalty."

She fluffed her hair and pouted. "Fine. But it *is* Friday night, Cal. Everyone goes out on Friday night. Even you."

"Don't you need to study on the weekends?" He wanted her to succeed in school. Moving from high school to college was a big step, especially for someone as young as Allison.

"Well, duh, that's the advantage of a high IQ." She flashed him a mischievous smile he hadn't seen since before their dad died. "Even we academic types need a little fun in our lives. Take Madeline Watson, for instance."

Guilt pounced him, making him feel like a kid caught with a girlie magazine. The last person he wanted to discuss with his sixteen-year-old sister was Maddy. Cal stood. "Maybe we better get to bed, Al. You must be exhausted."

Allison jumped to her feet, knocking her purse to the floor and scaring Duchess to the other side of the room. "I'm not exhausted, and it's not okay for you to change subjects midstream. If I'm going to get in trouble for breaking the rules, then I think I deserve a conversation about what happened and why I broke them." She folded her slender arms over her floral dress, a feisty contrast to her delicate clothes.

She took a deep breath and continued to rail, leaving Cal barely enough time to brace himself.

"I feel terrible about your car, but I'll pay you back, eventually. What I don't feel terrible about is breaking the stay-home-and-study rule on Friday night. I don't need to study, and you're robbing me of social growth opportunities."

This sounded a little too much like a conversation he'd had with a spunky sociology professor. If he didn't squelch it—fast—his little sister could be hitting the bars in spiked heels before he could say "teen rebellion."

Damn, parenting was proving as difficult as shaking his bad reputation.

"'Social growth'?" This was the drawback of having a genius for a sister. She always sounded as if she knew what she was talking about. "What kind of 'social growth' do you experience when you're running the roads at midnight in a pirated car?"

She stamped her foot. "I wouldn't have to pilfer a car if you'd help me buy a used one. Just because you choose to have no life since Katie left—"

"Wait a minute, sport—"

"It's true! You never go anywhere since she walked out. And even worse, you seem to think any woman you meet is going to be as unfeeling as Katie was."

"Don't you think you're getting a little bit off the subject here?" Cal took deep, calming breaths, reminding himself to not debate this subject with a teenager. Allison didn't know about all the women he'd dated since his ex-wife had fallen out of love with him as fast as she'd supposedly fallen into it. And he had no intention of her finding out how he'd earned his reputation on campus.

Allison's expression softened. "Sorry, Cal, I just think it needs saying. Just because *she* was too concerned with moving in the right social circles to see what a great guy you are doesn't mean the right woman isn't out there."

He would have snarled at anyone else who dared to spout marriage counselor wisdom at him, but he merely squeezed his sister's hand to let her know he'd heard the message.

And changed the subject before she could tell him anything else he didn't want to hear.

"Al, is it so much to ask you to put a little effort in your studies? Your education is your future." This was a safer topic—and one that was more important than she realized. Didn't she know how much an education could change her life? "You don't want to end up working as a mechanic, do you?"

She rolled her eyes with the drama only a sixteen year old can muster. "As if. And don't pretend you don't love fooling around under your cars. You could be the CEO of a national repair chain and you'd still find something to do in the grease pit every weekend."

He couldn't argue that point. But it didn't change the fact that his success had bought him a respect he never would have won if he'd stayed a simple mechanic. Too bad Katie hadn't stuck around long enough to see that he could do more than change tires.

Allison toyed with the locket around her neck. "Let's face it. I'm already excelling in school, so I don't need to be stuck in my room all weekend. I only want the privileges that my friends have."

Her words sounded reasonable enough. But maybe Cal was just overtired. This conversation—this night— had drained him more than an engine overhaul. "And if I give you more freedom, you'll keep up your grades?"

Nodding, she stepped toward him and clutched his arm. "Just think how well your friend Professor Watson balances her academic studies with her private life. I saw what she bought for this weekend, Cal, and let me tell you, she doesn't spend all her time studying." A flicker of admiration lit Allison's gaze.

Panic clenched his gut. His sister wanted to emulate Maddy? A few weeks ago he would have thought it a great idea. Now he cursed himself for ever introducing the two of them. If Madeline went out next week to trash her reputation with bad-girl antics, would Allison follow suit?

"Maybe not, but she studies a lot." That was one of the reasons he'd always admired Maddy. "And when she's not studying, she grades papers and develops her lesson plans."

Allison plucked at the folds of her skirt and sighed. "Maddy is smart, but she has a life, too. I don't."

Of all the people for his little sister to choose as a role model, she had to pick Maddy the Ticking Time Bomb, the woman whose inner bad girl was dying to get out.

He wiped a weary hand across his face and snapped his fingers to the dog. Thank God he could at least count on Duchess to be a stable female in his life.

"Just give me a few days to think about it, okay?" He scratched the dog's head and worked out a plan in his mind. "I'm sure we'll find a workable compromise."

Appeased, Allison retrieved her purse and headed up the stairs for bed while Cal went out to the garage to assess the damage on the Thunderbird.

As he ran his hands over the dented metal and scratched paint, Cal knew there was only one thing for him to do. Monday morning he'd have it out with Maddy. Putting her reputation on the line to make a point to her dissertation committee was a bad idea. Who knew how many students she would be influencing? If Allison noticed the changes in the Lady Scholar, certainly other people would.

Maybe his plan to show Maddy the nuances of seduction had been selfish. Had he just been giving himself permission to do what he'd longed for all these years? He'd be furious if some two-bit mechanic tried to make the moves on his innocent sister that he'd been contemplating with Maddy.

He took one last look at his battered car before shutting off the garage light and heading back to the house. He would give Madeline the courtship experience she needed for her mating rituals study, but he wouldn't engage in a physical relationship that could only hurt her in the end.

Somehow he'd have to convince Maddy to behave herself in public before she wreaked the kind of damage even he couldn't fix.

MADELINE HADN'T EXPECTED she'd need to perform damage control this early into her scheme, but here it was Monday morning and she was already on the receiving end of an outraged telephone call from her father.

She twisted the telephone cord around her thumb until she had a stack of coils wrapped from knuckle to fingernail, waiting for a break in his tirade about the indignity of professors who traipsed around campus in slinky red dresses.

Her office mate was teaching a class, so she had the space to herself for the next hour. She transferred grades from her students's papers to her grade book while her father threatened to come to town to talk some sense into her.

That caught her attention.

"Daddy, you don't want to come out here this time of year." She had to make sure he stayed safely ensconced on his own campus in upstate New York. Rensselaer Polytechnic Institute had been his professional domain and home turf since she was a child—the extent of his world except for the few colleges he visited for conferences and speaking engagements. "Louisville puts on a tiny physics conference anyway. You know that."

Her father would go berserk if he discovered she was trying to change her pristine reputation. Maybe because she was his only child, her father had high academic and personal expectations for her. Even a thousand miles away, the man knew if she was wavering from her course.

Of course, it helped that he had physics cronies at every major college in the U.S. and beyond. Apparently one of his scientist friends had been on campus Friday night to witness her scene with Cal and note all the details of her red dress.

She didn't think her father would really make good on his threat to visit her this weekend, but just the thought filled her with dread. She loved her dad, but sometimes she feared she disappointed him by not being as brilliant as he'd always been.

"Look, Dad, I have a class in five minutes," she lied, hoping to throw him off the scent. "The red dress was part of a sociology experiment, so don't worry about it."

At the sound of a discreet cough coming from the corridor, Madeline turned around.

She found the object of her experiment framed in her office door.

Lord, but Cal Turner's body deserved framing. She smiled and waved him in, hoping she could hide her nervousness after thinking about him and his offer all weekend.

"Dad, I've got to go now, but don't worry about me. I'll be fine. And you don't need to make a trip, I promise." She hustled her father off the phone, easing her conscience by telling herself she'd write another research paper soon to placate him, then turned to greet Cal.

"Hi." Her mind failed to come up with anything better on short notice.

"Hey, gorgeous." He pointed toward the chair opposite her. "You mind if I sit for a minute?"

Her heart rate kicked up as his knee brushed hers in the narrow space. He didn't teach today, and he normally never ventured on campus before five o'clock. Had he come to give her the private lessons they'd discussed?

He sank into the chair and leaned back, dominating her small office with his outstretched legs. Dressed in jeans and a T-shirt, she guessed he must be on his way to the garage. Madeline missed seeing him like this— the way he looked whenever she took her car in for service.

Hair still damp from his shower, he surveyed her with moody hazel eyes.

"Is everything all right?" She leaned closer, wondering if her new contact lenses were playing tricks on her. Cal had always seemed so carefree.

"So the red dress was just an experiment?" he asked, ignoring her question. He was watching her in a disconcerting way this morning, his direct gaze at odds with the playful man she'd known over the years.

She shrugged, unable to read his mood. "My dad's spies reported back to him already. He wants to come to the physics conference this weekend and check up on me for himself."

He nodded. "He'll be upset if he figures out what you are up to?"

"He just wants me to succeed in my field. He wouldn't think a dissertation on mating rituals was the best way to do that." Her father had always been a traditionalist, a man who played by the rules. Maddy was only just now beginning to realize she longed to break a few rules, to occasionally please herself instead of everyone else.

Cal leaned forward to rest his elbows on his knees, putting him a foot away from her. She wondered if he had any idea how his mere presence affected her.

"Do you think maybe you should just forget this whole scheme, Maddy?"

"Forget it?" Her voice cracked just a little, so she cleared her throat. "Why? Have you changed your mind?"

She held her breath, understanding for the first time how badly she wanted Cal Turner to be The One—the man to whom she lost her virginity.

He clamped one hand around each of her armrests and pulled her wheeled office chair over to his. "I'm going to court you like you've never been courted in your life, Madeline Watson. I meant, do you think you ought to skip the public display portion of your plan?"

"Absolutely not." Thanking the fates that Cal wasn't going to renege on their deal, she turned away from him to fish in her drawer for a contraband piece of bubble gum. She would need it for this conversation. "I've waited four years to do the kind of sociology projects I want to do and I'm not waiting any longer."

Snagging a pack of watermelon-flavored gum, she tossed half a piece in her mouth and offered one to Cal. He shook his head.

"Then why don't you just start pulling your resources together and do a thorough outline of your research strategies instead? You're a scholastic dynamo, woman." He gestured toward the mountain of books lining her walls. "You'll knock their socks off with a loaded proposal they can't turn down."

"They *can* turn it down, Cal. They already know I'm capable of putting together the paper trail." She straightened the items on her desk, trying to not reveal how much it had bothered her to have her dream project rejected. "What they don't know is whether or not I have the experience to add the human element to this study. I think they envision me as a sort of automaton."

Cal leaned back in his chair. "What makes you say that?"

"Isn't that how everybody sees me? I'm the department workhorse with no real passion or personality." She blew a bubble and popped it, wondering if Cal saw her that way, too. His detached manner worried her. "But I'm tired of it. I'm not living for my dad's approval anymore."

Cal shook his head. "Two rebel women in one week. I can't believe this."

She frowned. "What do you mean?"

"Allison is going rogue on me, too. She absconded

with one of my cars on Friday night and had a little fender bender."

"Is she okay?" Allison Turner had been through enough the past few months.

"She's fine, but she's ready to throw off the shackles of my expectations and live it up on the weekends now." Cal steepled his fingers and tapped them against his chin. "In fact, she named you as her inspiration to let loose."

"I'm sorry, Cal." Guilt stabbed her. She hadn't meant to share her penchant for a new lifestyle with anyone, least of all such an impressionable young woman as Allison. "I don't know why—"

"Maybe it had something to do with your lingerie choices at the mall last week," Cal volunteered, frustration lacing his words.

"I assure you, I concealed my lingerie choices from your sixteen-year-old sister." Madeline bristled. She had that much sense at least.

His brow furrowed. "Then what purchase did you show her after I left the store?"

"The red dress, of course." How could men be so obtuse? Then his answer clicked into place in her head. "But that might be why Allison thinks I'm hip all of a sudden. She loved the red dress."

Cal groaned. "Oh, great. The social services department will be really impressed with the home I provide for my sister when she starts parading around town in scarlet silk."

Madeline couldn't suppress a smile, much as she empathized with Cal's predicament. "It beats parading around in black lace."

"Depends who's wearing it." He met her gaze and held it, looking for all the world as though he knew exactly what she was wearing beneath her bulky shirt and cotton skirt.

"*I* might be wearing it if I find myself on the receiving end of a lesson in human mating rituals." A split second after the sentiment left her lips, Madeline wanted to call it back. She felt the flush start at her toes and move on to blister her whole body with heat.

Cal's gaze smoldered as it landed on her breasts. Although she remained well concealed beneath her shirt, she guessed she was currently very bare in his mind.

The notion thrilled her.

He shifted closer, surrounding her thighs with his in the narrow office. "Maddy, you don't want to tease me with black lace."

"Give me one good reason why."

"You'll definitely lose your shot at tenure when all of Fultz Hall hears you scream with the orgasm I give you."

7

EVERY NERVE ENDING screamed along with his threat, and he hadn't even touched her. Madeline's heart pummeled her chest, flooding her limbs with heat. She couldn't have nudged a word past her lips even if she had anything to say.

Cal looked almost as shocked at his words as she felt. His shallow, quick breaths seemed to pace her own.

He eased his chair back and stood. "I'm going to leave now before I do something we both regret. Maybe we can discuss this tomorrow, if you're free after class for date number two."

She nodded, watching him step through the door and into the hall.

"Good. I'll pick you up at nine." He leaned through the door to smile at her one more time. "And, Maddy?"

"Hmm?" The sound caught in her throat, rusty and awkward. She stared at his muscular forearm braced on the door frame.

"When the day comes that you find yourself on the receiving end of a lesson in mating rituals..." He lowered his voice another notch. "Let's skip the black lace altogether."

Madeline stared at the entrance Cal had just vacated, waiting for her breath to return. She remembered this feeling from elementary school—that moment you fell flat on your back from the monkey bars and knocked the wind clear out of your chest.

Only in elementary school there were no hormones or hard-bodied mechanics to complicate matters.

Her breathing had barely resumed when an efficient feminine voice sounded at the door.

"Knock, knock?"

Madeline shook herself in a vain attempt to ward off the leftover sizzle from Cal's visit. She tried to smile at Rose Marie, who stood at the door with a thin file folder in hand.

"Come on in."

Rose Marie edged her way into the room. "What's the matter, Maddy? Those flushed cheeks make you look like a guilty teenager caught in the act."

Madeline scooped her grade book off the desk and fanned herself. Rose Marie had no idea how dead-on her guess had nearly been. "Just hot in here, I think."

Rose Marie shrugged and continued to study Madeline. "You ditched the glasses?" She lifted Madeline's face to the light.

"What do you think?" Madeline couldn't quite get used to her new contact lenses, comfortable though they might be. She'd always liked the intelligent look of glasses, plus they gave her something to hide behind. She felt more exposed today wearing her contacts than she had on Friday night when she'd worn her red dress.

"I never knew you had such pretty eyes, but..."

"What?"

"I guess I'm just used to seeing you with glasses. It doesn't seem quite like you."

Madeline ceased her fanning and replaced her grade book on the desk, ready to carry on rational conversation now. "That's exactly how I feel. But I figure it makes a noticeable statement."

"And that's your main concern these days, isn't it?" Rose Marie dropped into the office chair opposite Madeline and slapped the file folder on the other desk. "You want to make a noticeable statement."

"Can you blame me?" Why were her friends giving her a hard time about this? Couldn't they see what she needed to accomplish? "I've got to do something to catch the university's attention before I get stuck doing two more years of literary sociology. I'm not backing down, Rose."

"Couldn't you compromise?" Rose Marie rapped her hand on the desk, causing her file to jump. "Find something less controversial than mating rituals and something more exciting than literary sociology?"

She'd thought of that, and dismissed it. "Sorry, Rose, but I've been compromising my whole life. I'm not settling for half measures this time."

"Very well." Rose Marie turned and retrieved the file folder on the desk in front of her. "Your request for a new dissertation hearing has been granted. I tried to give you as much time as I could, but the committee wants you to devote yourself to your project by the beginning of October. They want to hear your presentation two weeks from today."

"Two weeks?" Madeline croaked. How would she ever garner a more worldly reputation by then?

Handing the file to Madeline, Rose Marie stood and turned to leave. "Good luck finding a man to flaunt around campus, Maddy. Maybe you ought to talk to that gorgeous business teacher I saw walk out of your office not ten minutes ago. He looks like the kind of guy who could change a woman's reputation in a hurry."

Madeline's cheeks heated and she thought of her promise to Cal to keep things quiet. "We're just friends."

"Then maybe you're not using all your assets to your benefit, hon. If U of L didn't frown on relationships between graduate students and teachers, I'd urge you to get as close to that man as possible and see what happens." Winking, Rose shut the door behind her.

Madeline could either contemplate her friend's advice for enticing Cal or ruminate over the bleak news in the file in front of her.

Cal proved a far more tempting option. But if the dissertation committee wanted to reconvene in two weeks, Madeline needed to step up her plan of action.

That meant Cal Turner couldn't tease her with the promise of his teachings any longer. He would have to show her the finer points of the mating ritual as soon as possible—preferably tomorrow night on date number two.

Could she ever encourage him to show her that soon? She didn't know the first thing about seduction, but she vowed to try her best to make him notice her.

With any luck, Cal wouldn't be going home without her tomorrow night.

SO MUCH FOR HIS great plan to court Madeline Watson with a gentleman's restraint.

Cal glanced up at the clock during his class lecture and cursed himself for getting distracted by Maddy for the hundredth time since their office chat the day before. One more hour to go until their agreed-upon date, and he had no idea how he would make it until then.

Thankfully, his students were nodding and making notes, asking an occasional question. He couldn't be messing up too badly.

But his mind wasn't on business diversification strategies, the topic of the evening's class. No, the only thing Cal could think about was Maddy's teasing promise to wear black lace for him.

He rolled out an overhead projector and talked the class through a flowchart of his company's organizational structure. Perfect Timing had been in business for five years and already had five branches. Cal had grown his business from his talent with a socket wrench and the sheer force of his will, yet he couldn't seem to make himself behave for ten minutes around Madeline.

Where did he get off threatening her with mind-blowing orgasms? Hadn't he promised himself to keep their relationship on a courtship-only basis? He wanted to treat her gently, respectfully, the way a woman such as Maddy should be treated. Instead, he had found himself telling her to leave her panties in her dresser drawer.

Big mistake.

Now she would expect a new level of intimacy from their date tonight...something he had no business tangling with. No matter how badly Maddy thought she wanted to learn the steps of seduction, she wouldn't be happy with a man who couldn't possibly commit himself to her.

Cal wanted to save them both the heartache—and to maintain the friendship he valued. He'd never had a relationship in his life—including his marriage—that had been as rewarding as his friendship with Maddy, and he wasn't about to give it up for hotter-than-a-blowtorch sex.

When class ended, he called home to check on Allison, who promised she was already tucked in for the night with her copy of Nietzsche. A little light reading for the genius, he guessed.

Reassured, he clicked off the phone and wondered how to handle tonight. One thing he'd decided, he would take Maddy for a quick trip to see his newest addition to the Perfect Timing franchise. He'd never had a chance to ask her more about her interest in cars, and the idea intrigued him.

Besides, a glorified garage and car wash would be a safe, non-tempting place to take her—no beds in sight. After that, maybe they'd head over to hear a band in Butchertown and grab a couple of cappuccinos.

Nervous as a kid on his first date, Cal still had no idea how to backtrack from the sexual banter they'd exchanged just yesterday.

His only hope was that Maddy would be nervous, too, and would allow him to set the tone of their date. Maybe then he could treat her to the more civilized introduction to courtship and flirtation she deserved.

MADELINE ADJUSTED her black leather skirt and grimaced, wondering now if she'd gone a bit too far with her new ensemble.

She wanted to make an impression on Cal tonight, but even she wondered at the wisdom of trooping around town in her outfit. Sitting on her white linen duvet, she frowned down at her garb. The skirt exposed more thigh than most of her summer shorts and clung to her hips like an X-rated Band-Aid. Her silky top was semisheer, but more modest than the skirt. The black stilettos put her over the top, however, making her resemble a dominatrix more than a college professor.

Good.

If Cal had any reservations about what she wanted tonight, they would be lambasted the moment he caught a glimpse of her in this get-up.

She wanted that screaming orgasm.

Her doorbell rang and a tremor of pure excitement thrummed through her along with the Winchester chime. She switched off the bedroom light and forced herself to walk slowly down the hall. No sense twisting an ankle before she had the chance to cash in on Cal's volunteer to tutor her firsthand.

At the door she paused. Taking deep breaths, she tried to relax, to tell herself she wasn't nervous about making this next big step.

She was going out with Cal, after all. Her friend.

Gripping the knob with the steely determination that had driven her through eight years of higher education, Maddy opened the door to find the man who dominated her fantasies on the other side.

He wore a spotless version of jeans and boots, clothes that had obviously never seen the inside of the garage. He carried a white rose tied with a slender length of white satin.

Her heart lurched to see his gentlemanly offering. She didn't look fit to receive it in her showgirl garb.

"Hi." She realized she had crossed her feet in front of one another like some gangly teenager.

"Damnation, Maddy." He whispered the words while staring, wide-eyed, at her legs. A hint of backwoods Tennessee crept into his drawled oath.

How could she uncross her tangled feet now? Flushing with the heat of uneasiness and the sizzle of Cal's scrutiny, Madeline tried to interpret his reaction.

"You don't like it?"

His gaze finally reached her face and he gaped at her in what she could only guess was mild horror.

"How can I take you out in public when you're dressed in that, woman?" He edged his way inside, keeping plenty of distance between them.

She stepped forward to shut the door, effectively disengaging her legs. Willing her heart to quit pounding the heck out of her chest, she smiled. "You don't have to take me out if you don't want to."

She'd be more than happy to stay right here, with him.

He backed up a step, then thrust the rose between them as if it were a shield. "But I promised you a date. We can't just skip the rituals when the rituals are the whole point of your research, can we?"

She withdrew the flower from his fingers, touched by his thoughtfulness. "Thank you."

Too bad her seduction wasn't working. He wanted a formal date despite all her efforts.

She reached for the doorknob. "We can go out for a little while, if you want. We could head downtown to hear some music and—"

"No." He stepped between her and the door, bumping her leg as he did.

A quivery tingle danced in her veins at that accidental brush of bodies. What would it be like when he touched her for real?

"No way are you setting foot out of this house dressed like that." He folded his arms across his chest and settled against the door frame as if he planned to guard the exit all night.

Why wasn't he responding to her loud-and-clear signals? Had she misjudged his interest? His intent?

No. How could you misinterpret such a statement as "let's skip the black lace"?

This called for more forceful measures. Apparently, Cal needed greater incentive to take her in his arms and not let go until she knew all there was to know about mating.

She sidled up to him as close as she could without touching him. "Then I guess that means we'll have to stay in all night. Just you and me..."

Cal tugged his shirt collar. "Maybe we should at least go over to the garage."

"The garage?" She all but shrieked. She was hell-bent on seduction and he wanted to take her to his repair shop?

"A brand-new Perfect Timing I'm opening next weekend." He flashed her a lopsided grin as he slid out from between her and the door. "It'll be the cleanest garage you've ever seen. Nice body shop. New car wash..."

She thought she heard him mutter something about "and no beds" under his breath, but she was too mad to be sure. She tapped the rose against her thigh in an agitated rhythm.

Then, recalling that his romantic offering marked her first flower from a man, she paused to take an appreciative sniff. Maybe a trip to the garage would be okay.

"How...nice." She couldn't believe she was failing so miserably in her scheme. How would she ever learn anything about mating rituals from Cal if he insisted on dragging her all over town to see hydraulic lifts?

He peered around the room expectantly. "Have you got a coat?"

"No." She marched to the door and stepped outside, not bothering to see if he followed.

Madeline Seduces a Man, Part Two, was about to begin, and she would make sure this phase went a lot smoother than the debacle in her front hall just now. Of course, no sooner had she told herself as much when she promptly turned her ankle in her skyscraper heels.

Accepting Cal's arm to steady her, she righted her shaky balance and determination.

She slid into Cal's car and slammed the door behind her. While she waited for him to get in, she took deep, relaxing breaths and willed herself to think. What had Rose Marie suggested?

Get as close to that man as possible and see what happens.

Madeline maneuvered to the middle of the bench seat just as Cal got inside.

Their thighs converged, hip to knee. The rush of heat that blazed through her infused her with courage, made her more confident in her plan.

As Cal backed the Chevy on to the street, she whispered to him. "Isn't there supposed to be a second date kiss?"

His jaw flexed, calling her attention to the light shadow of stubble on his cheek.

"Honey, I'm the one with the experience here, right?"

His foot switched from the gas to the brake at a stoplight, shifting his thigh against hers. The scratch of his jeans against her barely-there stockings stoked a hunger she'd only recently become aware of.

She turned toward him a bit more and leaned to breathe her response into his ear. "But you forgot the second date kiss."

She took the opportunity of the stopped car to graze her lips against the soft scratch of his cheek. On impulse, she stole a quick taste of his warm skin.

He let out a low whistle between his teeth as he started the car forward again. "Honey, you don't know what that does to me."

The dark intimacy of the car interior compelled her to confide her real thoughts. "I wish it did more."

Abruptly he pulled over to the side of the road, oblivious to the potholes the Chevy trounced over to get there. He threw the gearshift into Park and turned on her.

"Do you mean that, Madeline Watson, or are you

just tempting the hell out of me as some kind of social experiment?"

She considered his words before responding—no easy task with his body mere inches from hers.

His hazel eyes glimmered dark and dangerous in the close atmosphere of the car. She realized in that moment something that had always fascinated her about this man—his primal earthiness called to a part of herself she'd never before confronted.

"I want you as more than a social experiment, Cal."

"You do?" He was giving her an out, a way to still take her stilettos and run.

She didn't want to.

Maddy trailed a fingertip down his cheek. "I want to see how fast we can go from zero to sixty in that back seat of yours."

8

CAL HAD GOTTEN INTO more than his fair share of slug-fests in life, but no one had ever packed a punch like the one Madeline had just landed with her outrageous proposal.

He gritted his teeth, determined to not rush head-long into something they would regret. "You deserve better than a back seat, Maddy. No matter how high the heels or how short the skirt, you're still as respect-able as they come."

"And just look where respectable has gotten me—a rejected dissertation and a career hanging in the bal-ance. Not to mention that at this rate I'll be the only doctoral graduate with virginity intact. No job. No life. I don't want to play it safe anymore." Her brown eyes loomed, wide and entreating without the barrier of her glasses.

Cal knew his defenses against her were running low. God knew, he was trying his damnedest to do this the honorable way. Could he help it if the Lady Scholar had a bad-girl streak a mile wide?

Then an idea blindsided him. A surefire way to make Madeline see they were all wrong for each other. All he had to do was get her to his car shop.

He cupped her chin in his palm, not trusting himself to touch any part of her but her heart-shaped face.

"Honey, you've achieved more in twenty-five years than most people do in a lifetime. Don't sell yourself short."

She bit her lip and said nothing, but she couldn't hide the obvious disappointment in her eyes. Cal wondered how in the hell she had ever convinced herself that a spruced-up mechanic like him was right for a blue-blood academic like her.

But soon, she would understand the truth.

"I'm taking you out on the date you deserve, Maddy. But I want to show you one thing first." He shifted the car into gear and eased back onto the road. "We're only two blocks from the new shop."

"We're still going to your garage?" Maddy's voice threaded through the car, her tone betraying only a hint of frustration.

Cal watched her via the dashboard lights. Her hand fluttered toward her face, and she reached to push the glasses up on her nose that were no longer there.

"It's not just a garage," he explained, anxious to prove to her why their worlds were light-years apart. "It's a car salon." He pulled into the dark parking lot and killed the ignition.

She hopped out of his Chevy before he could get the door for her. He loved it that she seemed oblivious to the most basic dating conventions. She might be a brilliant sociology teacher, but he'd been the first man to teach her anything about relationships between men and women.

"I'm glad to see your latest business, Cal, really I am." She tugged at the hem of her outfit, luring his attention to her legs with their barely-there stockings. "But I'm still hoping for a lesson tonight."

From any other woman, the comment would have sounded coy. Not so when the words fell from Madeline Watson's naive lips. "Not a chance I could forget, Maddy."

Unwilling to touch her for fear he wouldn't stop, he headed for the front door and unlocked it. Her heels clicked a seductive rhythm across the parking lot as she caught up with him. For a moment, he imagined her fingers walking up his chest with the same languorous beat. She sidled past him over the threshold, kicking up his heart rate by several blood-pounding notches. She smelled like raspberries and the bubble gum she seemed to have a secret penchant for.

"There's a paint shop inside!" Maddy exclaimed, her gaze lighting upon the wall full of color cards. "And a car wash!"

He studied her as she rushed over to touch the rainbow of paint cans, surprised that her appreciation seemed genuine.

"We can do anything from an oil change to a broken windshield repair." Cal pointed to a couple of the big bays across from the paint area. "We can also fix an older car's carburetor or a new car's fancy computer chip." He ducked behind the front counter while she spun around to take it all in. "Then we send you on your way with a wash and wax job."

He pushed the button for the automated car wash and let her take in the glory of Perfect Timing's showpiece. Through a pane of glass, the whole reception area could view the state-of-the-art system of spraying water, foaming pink bubbles and spouting yellow wax. The soft brushes spun like a carnival ride, dipping and swirling in their search for a vehicle to clean.

Cal knew other people wouldn't be as enthused about his business as him—especially not the Lady Scholar, whose whole world revolved around her academics and research. Perfect Timing represented a dream fulfilled for him, but Maddy would only see a car wash.

"Wow!" She pivoted to look at him, her eyes reflecting the same delight he'd felt when he'd first eyed this contraption. "It could be right out of *Willie Wonka!*"

God help him. She seemed to think it was as cool as he did. Pride sang through him at her words, along with a renewed dose of lust for a woman who could appreciate his invention.

He left the machine running and came out from behind the counter to join her, inordinately pleased and terrified that the professor gave good grades to something besides research papers. "I put together the specs for it and submitted it to an architect. I couldn't believe the guy made it all work just the way I'd described."

"*You* thought of this?"

The tenuous barrier he'd erected between them crumbled in the face of the admiration shining in her eyes. He nodded, now knowing he'd never be able to say no to this woman. "My mother calls it daydreaming," he confided.

Maddy turned to him, a mischievous smile playing at her lips. "They say if you can dream it, you can do it."

"I guess so." He moved to shut off the machine. His

mission to send her running might have been a dismal failure, but now he could have his night with her. He couldn't deny what he felt for her any longer, and he sure as hell couldn't wait to get her out of here and satisfy every erotic desire Madeline Watson ever had.

Madeline's voice stopped him cold. "Do you want to try it out?"

His hand hovered over the button, allowing the car wash to continue its colorful dance. Disappointment crowded his chest as he pivoted back to her. He wanted her so bad he could almost taste those bubble gum lips of hers. He didn't want to wait. "You can pull the Chevy inside if you want, but—"

She grabbed his hand and tugged him toward the car wash service entrance. "No. I mean, do *you* want to try it out."

"You're kidding." The hum of the machinery increased as they neared the door. The buzz of blood in his veins seemed to throb right along with it.

For the first time since he'd picked her up at her doorstep, he allowed his gaze to travel slowly up her legs and over her curves in the dim lights of the reception desk. The professor wanted love lessons?

Well, by God, he'd do his best to make sure he taught her well before she found herself another tutor. No way would he let this sweet woman fall into the hands of some slam-bam-thank-you-ma'am clod.

She flashed him her A-plus grin, making his mouth go dry as chalk dust. Her faith in him was a bracing reminder that this woman wasn't just another fling. No matter how scientifically professor Maddy approached this business of seduction, nothing would ever be the same between them after tonight. He had to make their time together something she would never, ever forget.

"What about tonight's lesson in seduction?" He had been wanting to touch her for four years. He didn't think he could wait for her any longer.

At the door, she paused. She looked up at him with her most infectious bad-girl grin. "I've decided there would be nothing more seductive than to learn among pink bubbles."

Oh, God. Where on earth did Little Miss Innocent come up with erotic ideas like this one? He waited for a moment, trying to envision how he could accommodate her without getting them both killed by twirling brushes.

"Please?"

Her soft request undid him, made him ready to slay dragons or heavy car wash equipment if need be. He leaned over her, powerless to keep his hands off her another minute.

Her eyes closed when his hand brushed around her waist, tangling in the length of her silky brown hair. She slid slender arms around his neck. Cal braced himself on the glass door behind her, the thrum of the machines vibrating though the barrier and up his arms to shake his whole world.

Her lips tilted toward him. He wanted nothing more than to accept that tempting offer and to lose himself in her kiss, but first he would make sure this was one lesson she'd never forget. He scooped her off her feet, into his arms and backed them through the service door.

The rinse cycle got them right away, spraying over Maddy's leg and Cal's hand, but it didn't begin to douse the heat her soft curves inspired. For a little thing, she was an armful.

"Cal!" she cried his name between fits of laughter.

"Too late now, Professor." He spoke the words into her ear so she could hear him over the noise. "You're all mine."

Her body went still. Her giggles evaporated, their sound replaced by the clank of Cal's boots on the metal-grate walkway alongside the machinery. They would be safe on the narrow passage, but they'd be plenty wet by the time they were through.

Cal strode through a mist of water toward the soap cycle. When they neared the nozzles spraying pink bubbles, she wiggled in his arms.

"Stop here." She reached for one of the foaming jets before he could put her down, grazing his forearm with a tantalizing brush of silk-covered breasts. She evidently had no idea what kind of torture she wreaked with her movements. "Gotcha."

Before he knew what she was about, she'd blasted his chest with suds, plastering his T-shirt to his skin.

"I could spray you back pretty easily." He glanced down at her weapon and then stared meaningfully at the enticing target her chest would make. The heavy mist in the air already made her blouse cling to the lacy bra she wore beneath. "But I think I'll take my revenge another way."

He flicked the hose out of her hand. As it flew back into position, it spewed froth in every direction, covering his back and her legs with soap. He backed her up against the wall, shielding her from the worst of the light rain with his body. Slowly he eased her to her feet, making sure he planted her high heels safely away from the grates in the floor.

Maddy moaned low in her throat as he slid his hands up the sides of her slippery thighs. He paused at the leather of her skirt, teasing one finger along her hem in lazy circles. Her fingers clenched his shoulders, and she swayed on her tiny heels.

"Please, Cal." She whispered the words. Yet he was so close to her now, so attuned to her reactions, he detected every nuance of her voice despite the thunderous machines.

"Revenge, in this case, is far from sweet." He slipped his hands beneath her skirt and cupped her hips. He pulled her against him, molding her to him. His mind registered the fact that she'd neglected to wear the black lace panties, but if he thought about it for long, he would never finish the lesson.

The full body contact, even clothed, sapped his brain cells and fired his blood to a painful degree. The cool water didn't make a dent in the heat between them.

"You can just take all the revenge you want." She hitched his T-shirt up and splayed red-tipped fingers across his chest. "I've got all night."

"Honey, you don't have a clue what you're offering me." Cal pulled his shirt over his head and tossed it to the floor, but he hesitated over the buttons to her wet blouse.

She tipped her chin at him. "I think I might." She leaned into him, teasing him with the fullness of her breasts.

Wet denim became his hated enemy. It occurred to him he was more hot for her than he'd ever been for any other woman, and he hadn't even kissed her yet tonight.

He traced the outline of her lips with one finger. Jets of water streamed full-speed into his back, urging him to part her thighs and lose himself inside her. But a woman like Madeline deserved thorough appreciation. He hadn't worshiped her the way he wanted to, yet she seemed to be on fast forward along with his libido. On his next lap around her mouth, Maddy pulled his finger between her lips and gently sucked the tip.

He'd have to save worshiping for their next time together, damn it. He didn't have the power to fight Maddy if she was hell-bent on seduction.

"Tell me this is what you want." Cal undid her buttons with fingers long accustomed to manipulating the most delicate of engines. Her wet bra clung to her curves for less than a blink before he flicked that away, too.

"This is what I want," Maddy replied, her clear brown gaze tinged with desire but aware enough to know what she said.

Needing no further urging, Cal turned to catch a handful of bubbles. He held them over her body for a long moment, until she squirmed just a little. Then he spread them over her breasts, being careful to evenly distribute the suds between them.

Her nipples seemed to peek through no matter how diligently he covered them up. Or perhaps he just had a good eye for them. He scraped away a little patch of foam to taste one.

Maddy's fingers clawed through his hair. Who would have guessed she'd hidden such a craving for

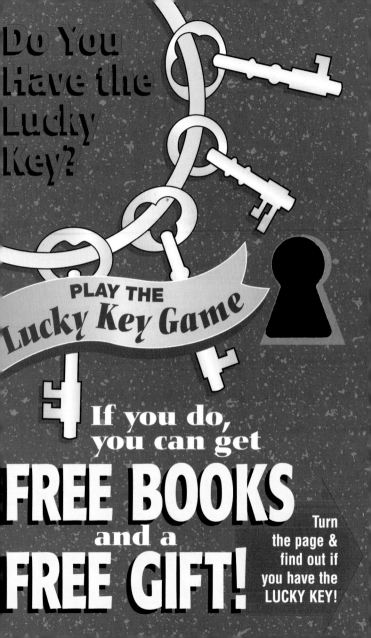

PLAY THE
Lucky Key Game

and get

HOW TO PLAY:

1. With a coin, carefully scratch off gold area at the right. Then check the claim chart to see what we have for you — **2 FREE BOOKS** and a **FREE GIFT** — **ALL YOURS FREE!**

2. Send back the card and you'll receive two brand-new Harlequin Temptation® books. These books have a cover price of $3.99 each in the U.S. and $4.50 each in Canada, but they are yours to keep absolutely free.

3. There's no catch. You're under no obligation to buy anything. We charge nothing —ZERO — for your first shipment. And you don't have to make any minimum number of purchases — not even one!

4. The fact is, thousands of readers enjoy receiving books by mail from the Harlequin Reader Service®. They enjoy the convenience of home delivery...they like getting the best new novels at discount prices, BEFORE they're available in stores...and they love their *Heart to Heart* subscriber newsletter featuring author news, horoscopes, recipes, book reviews and much more!

5. We hope that after receiving your free books you'll want to remain a subscriber. But the choice is yours — to continue or cancel, any time at all! So why not take us up on our invitation, with no risk of any kind. You'll be glad you did!

YOURS FREE!
A SURPRISE GIFT

We can't tell you what it is...but we're sure you'll like it! A
FREE GIFT—
just for playing the LUCKY KEY game!

Visit us online at
www.eHarlequin.com

The Harlequin Reader Service® — Here's how it works:

Accepting your 2 free books and gift places you under no obligation to buy anything. You may keep the books and gift and return the shipping statement marked "cancel." If you do not cancel, about a month later we'll send you 4 additional books and bill you just $3.34 each in the U.S., or $3.80 each in Canada, plus 25¢ shipping & handling per book and applicable taxes if any.* That's the complete price and — compared to cover prices of $3.99 each in the U.S. and $4.50 each in Canada — it's quite a bargain! You may cancel at any time, but if you choose to continue, every month we'll send you 4 more books, which you may either purchase at the discount price or return to us and cancel your subscription.

*Terms and prices subject to change without notice. Sales tax applicable in N.Y. Canadian residents will be charged applicable provincial taxes and GST.

If offer card is missing write to: Harlequin Reader Service, 3010 Walden Ave., P.O. Box 1867, Buffalo NY 14240-1867

BUSINESS REPLY MAIL
FIRST-CLASS MAIL   PERMIT NO. 717-003   BUFFALO, NY

POSTAGE WILL BE PAID BY ADDRESSEE

HARLEQUIN READER SERVICE
3010 WALDEN AVE
PO BOX 1867
BUFFALO NY 14240-9952

NO POSTAGE
NECESSARY
IF MAILED
IN THE
UNITED STATES

carnal pleasures beneath the tweed jackets she'd worn just last week?

Tenderness for that woman, the one he'd admired even without the miniskirts, made him seek out her lips for a long, lazy, liquid kind of kiss. She tasted like bubble gum and soap. She was heaven incarnate.

"I need you now, Maddy." He felt it only right to warn her. This wasn't exactly what he'd had in mind for a seduction, but now that they'd started, he'd sell his soul along with Perfect Timing and all five of his antique cars if she'd only let him complete this quest for bliss.

"I think I need you more. I have protection in my purse."

He was so grateful for her willingness he would have pounded down the door of every convenience store in town if need be. He retrieved her miniature leather satchel from where it had fallen. "You are blessedly prepared, sweetheart. Just stay right there."

Shucking the jeans he'd come to hate, Cal kicked free the last of his clothing and sheathed himself. He lifted Maddy and her stilettos right off the ground. Wrapping one of her legs around each of his hips, he knew a moment of absolute satisfaction when she locked her heels behind his back.

All traces of nervousness from earlier in the evening had vanished. The student became the teacher as she squeezed her legs tightly around him and shimmied her hips over his erection.

A low moan rumbled through him, along with a powerful urge to possess Maddy in every way known to man. Her slick heat lured him, made him burn with a need so fierce it scared him.

"I'll try to not hurt you," he whispered, backing her against the wall. He steeled himself as he positioned her over him, determined to make her first time wonderful for her.

"Not a chance." Maddy framed his face with her hands and held his gaze for a long moment before she plunged downward.

At her slight wince, Cal knew a moment's regret that he hadn't initiated her in a more gentle way. Then he lost all ability to think or regret as she seemed to recover with remarkable speed, if her alluring wriggles against him were any indication. He held still for as long as he could, then lifted her just a little.

The squeal she made encouraged him.

Cool water and pink bubbles continued to pelt him, but they sizzled off the heat of his back. His blood scorched his veins, his pulse pounded in his temples to a dull roar, and he couldn't hold Maddy close enough. He lifted her up and pulled her back down the length of him, seeking a completion he feared he wouldn't find in just one night with her.

He touched her burning point, slipped his fingers across the taut heat of her where their bodies met. She arched back like a bow, offering herself to him until he found a rhythm that reverberated through them both.

Her body shuddered around his in waves, and he followed her in moments.

Cal held her throughout another rinse cycle, unable to move. Finally, she slid away from him and straightened her skirt.

"Wow."

Her lone comment pleased him more than a litany of praise. He couldn't wait to take her home and slide between the sheets of her bed for more rock-the-world mating lessons.

He retrieved his jeans and dressed, stealing occasional glimpses of her as she adjusted her blouse and stockings. God, she was gorgeous.

As he stepped into his boots, he leaned over to kiss her on the forehead. "You ready for a few more rounds like that one?"

"Are you kidding?" She peeled off her heels and grinned up at him like a kid who'd just blown her whole allowance on bubble gum. "I've got enough material now for a whole paper."

Cal tried to not wince at the blow to his ego. They'd just practically reinvented sex and apparently she'd been too busy taking notes to realize it. "Ah. That was good research then?"

"The best." She arched up on her toes to kiss him on the cheek, but Cal didn't know that he was in the mood for any more kissing—or research—tonight. He had been so concerned Maddy might get hurt if they initiated a physical relationship that he'd never stopped to consider what it might do to him.

And somehow tonight, in the unlikely heaven of his Perfect Timing shop, Cal had apparently been seduced by the master teacher.

9

TWO DAYS AFTER her soapy initiation into womanhood, Madeline scrounged through her office desk drawer in a frantic search for her last stash of caramels. She had three hours until her afternoon class and—with thoughts of Cal still plaguing her—she needed more chewing satisfaction than mere gum could provide.

Digging through paper clips and old file folders, Madeline wondered for the umpteenth time what had gone wrong the other night. What had started out as the most earth-moving evening of her life had rapidly deteriorated into the most awkward. And somehow, it had been all her fault.

Spying the familiar bag of her all-time-favorite treat, Madeline seized it and tore into the candy. Maybe if she allowed herself the luxury of devouring the whole bag, she would stop thinking about the way Cal had slowly retreated into long silences on the return trip to her house that night.

She traced the problems back to the aftermath of their car wash encounter. Everything had been going well until she'd told him how inspiring his lesson had been. What man wouldn't be flattered to hear that?

Of course, maybe she hadn't precisely said she'd been inspired. She tapped her temple with a pencil, trying to recall the exact conversation. Maybe she'd said something about him giving her a wealth of material to use for her research paper.

Another comment that should have flattered him, right?

Madeline looked down at the empty wrappers on her desk blotter. Six caramels into her binge and she still felt as miserable as she had when she'd started.

A niggling voice in the back of her mind told her why. Maybe Cal hadn't wanted to hear about her research paper five minutes after consummating their relationship.

Hadn't her parents' divorce taught her anything? Her mother hadn't wanted to hear about her father's adventures in physics every day. She especially didn't want to hear about it in light of the modest salary he made before he reached full professorship.

Normal people didn't enjoy being around absent-minded scholars like her and her father, who lived, breathed and slept their work. Which only confirmed what she had known all along—she and her sociology research didn't belong in a relationship with a man. From the time she'd entered her graduate program, she had slated her twenties as the time of her life to dedicate to her job. Maybe once she'd carved out an academic niche for herself, she'd have time for a man.

She swept the caramel bag off her desktop and back into the drawer in disgust. Of course her life hadn't fallen neatly into the plan she'd created. But then, she didn't ever have much luck fitting into people's plans for her.

She'd disappointed her dad by not entering a "real" science field. She'd frustrated her university superiors by not sticking with the type of sociology she'd always excelled at in the past. And she had probably disappointed Cal by talking about her dissertation project five minutes after the most profound experience of her life instead of telling him how incredible he'd made her feel.

Of course, she had probably retreated to blabbering about her projects because work was her comfort zone. She had been nervous and unsure of herself in the awkward moments following their provocative union.

No wonder he had dropped her off at her doorstep without coming inside. She'd unwittingly offended the man who'd been her closest friend four years running. Her mistake seemed all the more disgraceful considering Cal had tried his best to keep things platonic between them.

Madeline stared down at the blank notebook she'd planned to use for recording her impressions of the final step in the mating ritual. To write about what had happened between her and Cal seemed crass now, an act bound to cheapen an encounter that had awed her in its raw power.

She closed the notebook and slid it to the side of her desk, vowing she would not tarnish her night with Cal any more than she already had. Sooner or later, she would find a way to confront him and apologize.

With any luck, she could salvage their friendship. A more intimate relationship, however, was out of the question. Academic nerds like Madeline just weren't cut out for normal social interactions with people.

A young woman's voice at the door provided welcome relief from her depressing thoughts.

"Um...Professor Watson?"

Madeline turned to find Cal's brainy sister, Allison Turner, at her office door. A throng of students clogged the hallway behind her, indicating the end of a class period.

"Come on in, Allison." Madeline noted the girl's blond braids and the colored beads spanning her neck and wrists. She wore a tie-dyed shirt and embroidered jeans with a little peace sign stitched on one knee. Apparently Allison had ditched her cowgirl phase for the hippie look. "And, please, let's not be formal. You can call me Madeline."

Allison smiled. "Thanks. I'll only just be a minute, and I'm sorry to bother you." She closed the door behind her and sank into one of the office chairs, dropping her denim backpack beside her on the floor.

She had the same ready smile as Cal, and maybe the same cheekbones, but the resemblance ended there. Allison's blue eyes and blond mane must have come from her mother. She had a cool, Nordic look, compared to Cal's golden brawn and tawny hair.

"Take all the time you need." Madeline swiveled around to face her guest, wishing she could ask about Cal. "No one ever comes to see me during office hours until mid-semester grades are released."

Except for Cal, of course. He had sat here on Monday morning, his long legs brushing against hers....

"It's about Cal."

Madeline sat straighter. "What about him?"

Allison tucked one silvery braid behind her ear. "He's been a bear all week and he won't tell me what gives." Her brow furrowed. "Did he say anything to you the other night when you guys went out?"

"Well, uh, no. Come to think of it, he didn't."

Cal's sister folded her arms over her tie-dyed shirt and frowned. "If he said anything about me—like that I'm really disappointing him or something—I wish you'd let me in on it."

Madeline shook her head. "Definitely not. We didn't talk about you specifically the other night, but I know for a fact he's not disappointed with you in the least." She leaned forward and gave Allison's hand a quick squeeze of encouragement. No doubt, the poor girl had been through a year of turmoil.

Allison clutched Madeline's hand as if it were a lifeline. "But how do you know? He's barely said three words the past two days, Madeline. I think he's mad because I sneaked out of the house Friday and crashed the Thunderbird."

"I'm positive he's not angry with you." No, Cal was mad because Madeline had acted like an insensitive dweeb, but she didn't want to get into that topic with Cal's sixteen-year-old sister. "Cal has a Thunderbird, too?"

"A fifty-eight, I think." Allison nodded absently. "He's just been so moody and quiet."

A fifty-eight? Madeline wondered where he found these gems. If it was in half as nice shape as the Chevy, Cal's business obviously turned a handy profit.

She thought about Allison's words, wishing she could help her. "Sometimes, when my dad acts like that, I just do a lot of extra talking to make up for him."

Allison's blue eyes narrowed. "That works?"

"Sure it does!" Madeline grasped a topic that might break Allison's grip. "I'm an expert at gabbing my way around unresponsive men."

"Great! You can come have lunch with us and defuse the tension." Allison jumped up and tugged Madeline's captive arm.

"What?" Fear weighted Madeline to her chair. The cowgirl-turned-hippie hadn't seriously proposed Madeline go see Cal *now*, had she?

"Cal said he'd swing by to have lunch with me today, but I'm scared we'll go somewhere and just stare at our club sandwiches for an hour."

The hippie genius stared down at her with pleading blue eyes, looking just like the mischievous little sister Madeline would have gladly traded all her books for as a child.

She had to face Cal sometime, didn't she?

"Okay," Madeline agreed, allowing Allison to pull her to her feet. "But I do have a class this afternoon."

Allison beamed. "You'll be back in plenty of time, I promise." She gave Madeline a quick hug and giggled. "Wait till Cal sees I've got you with me!"

Madeline grabbed her purse and followed Allison out the door, thinking her bag of caramels would have made a much nicer meal than the awkward lunch to which she had just consigned herself. "He'll be surprised, all right."

"And pleased!" Allison added, linking arms with Madeline as though they were old friends. "I just know he'll be in a better mood after he sees you."

FOR THE FIRST TIME since he'd dropped Madeline off at her door Tuesday night, Cal thought he might have a shot at improving his dark mood.

He drove to the Louisville campus in a late-model Chevy spiffed up for Allison, a surprise gift she would flip over. This would definitely warrant a Brother of the Year award.

He just needed to make sure he didn't somehow run into the Lady Scholar and botch this tentative attempt to be agreeable. Allison's happiness was too important for him to spoil it with his love life woes.

He'd agreed to meet Allison at *The Thinker* statue at the main entrance. The horseshoe-shaped driveway made the perfect place for him to pull up curbside with his gift.

After much debate since the weekend, Cal had decided he'd be better served giving Allison a little more freedom instead of taking some away. She had a point about not being able to go out on the weekends. She worked diligently enough all week that she deserved an outing or two without her big brother breathing down her neck.

He didn't want to squelch her "social growth opportunities," after all. Maddy had been denied that sort of frivolity as a teenager, and look where it had landed her—with a penchant for leather and a talent for tempting well-meaning men to forsake all their morals.

Damn. He hadn't meant to get riled about the car wash episode again.

Today would be Allison's day. No Madeline thoughts to tease, tantalize or aggravate him.

He turned into the university's main entrance, easily maneuvering around the limited traffic. The quiet, tree-lined drive didn't connect to any major parking lots, existing more for show than utility. Cal appreciated the traditional collegiate look of this side of campus, especially the bronze cast of *The Thinker* statue.

Seeing this view of U of L's stately brick buildings made him remember why he'd been so proud to be offered a teaching position here. He'd spent enough time in the grease pits to consider life in the academic world pretty lofty.

He spied Allison and her flower-child clothes right away. He had already laid on the horn when he realized who his little sister was walking across campus with.

Madeline Watson. The woman who thought his sexual prowess ought to be chronicled in her dissertation.

The same woman who'd unwittingly trashed feelings he hadn't even realized he possessed for her.

Both Maddy and Allison turned toward the car horn, along with fifteen other people crossing campus. Briefly he thought of continuing right on past them and postponing his lunch with his sister, but that would be selfish.

He hadn't spent enough time with Allison since the night Madeline had knocked his world clear off its axis. He didn't want his sister to think he was avoiding her.

Besides, he'd gone to a lot of trouble to secure a nice car for her. He refused to let what had happened between him and Maddy spoil his enjoyment of the moment.

He would simply focus on Allison, and Madeline would go her own way once she learned Cal had a lunch date with his sister. He could endure five minutes in Maddy's presence without going back on his vow to not touch her again, couldn't he?

It was only five minutes.

"Allison!" Cal called out the window and waved his arm. He pulled into a vacant space on the wide curve of the access road.

His sister spied him and tugged Maddy along behind her.

Cal's no-touch resolve faltered just a little when he realized she was back to wearing her bulky men's shirts and long skirts. Black leather and heels had its appeal, but Cal had gotten fired up by tweed and button-downs long before lace and stilettos had come along.

With any luck, maybe it wouldn't take a whole five minutes for Allison to say goodbye to her teacher.

"Hey, Cal!" Allison reached the car and leaned in the passenger window, her pale blond braids hanging down like puppy dog ears. "Are you stealing loaner cars from the garage again?" she teased.

"Not a chance, doll." He hopped out of the car and nodded at Madeline as she glided to a halt beside his sister.

The Lady Scholar straightened the eyeglasses she was wearing once again.

Cal felt an electric jolt clear to his toes.

"Don't tell me you got this to replace your Thunderbird," Allison commented, idly running her finger over the hood. "I can't picture you in something so tame."

"Well, I hope you can picture *you* in it." He pulled a

little red ribbon from his pants pocket and slapped it on the car's shiny white roof. "It's just for you, sis."

Allison frowned. Her genius mind was slow putting together the meaning of his words, but Madeline seemed to have figured it out right away. Cal couldn't help the rush of pride he experienced when Maddy smiled her approval across the hood.

"You're kidding," Allison finally managed to say.

"Gee whiz, girl, show a little more faith in your big brother." He ushered Allison around the car, being careful to not get within raspberry range of Maddy. Opening the driver's side door, he nudged his sister inside. "You think I'm just going to let all the great social growth opportunities in life pass you by while you sit at home with me every weekend?"

Cal noticed Maddy start backing away, and silently applauded her sensitivity. He didn't need to be distracted by her sexy sensible shoes at a time when he should be reaping mega doses of sisterly love and gratitude.

"Oh, God, Cal. Thank you!" Allison leaped from the car and almost knocked him over with a bear hug. She turned around to call over her shoulder. "Maddy, do you believe this? Maddy! Come see my new car."

So much for Madeline's sly getaway. Damn. His palms already itched with the need to span her little waist and pull her curvy body to his.

Allison let him go to pull Madeline closer. "Can you believe it?" She hugged Maddy too, and then bounded back to her new car like a kid at Christmas. "Can I take it for a ride?" she asked, already toying with the keys.

Cal barely had time to say yes when she started it up and with exaggerated precision pulled on her seat belt.

"I'll just go around the block, okay?" She adjusted her mirrors and seat.

Cal nodded, then realized that would leave him standing here—alone—with the biggest temptation of his life. "Or else you can just drive us to lunch—"

Allison shook her head, already slipping the car in gear. "I want to eat on campus so we're not late for Maddy's class."

Oh, no. That didn't mean what he thought it meant, did it?

Fearing the worst, Cal reached for the passenger door, but Allison was pulling out into the driving lane.

"Madeline is coming with us!" she called through the open window as she drove away.

Leaving Cal and Madeline together. Alone.

Memories of their awkward drive home Tuesday night drifted back to him. He didn't really want to alienate the woman who had been a good friend to him, but if she insisted on wreaking havoc with his control and then knocking him flat with her scholarly critique of his performance, he didn't have a choice. He had to keep his head on straight to secure Allison's guardianship.

And maybe even his self-respect.

Madeline cleared her throat in a deliberate way, like a teacher trying to gain class attention. Cal figured she'd found an excuse to beg off the lunch date.

"I've been meaning to apologize for the other night." She peered up at him through her glasses, her eyes veiled by the reflected glare of the sun. Her hair twined around itself in a halfhearted coil at the back of her head.

To all the rest of the world, she might look like a frazzled professor who didn't put much emphasis on her appearance. But Cal saw the temptress. The wild child.

Even worse, he saw his friend.

"Maddy, you don't need to—"

She surprised him by barreling right over his words. "Yes, I do." She straightened her glasses, a gesture that, today, looked less like nervousness and more like gutsy determination.

She took a deep breath. "I was so...overwhelmed the other night that I might have blurted out some awkward remarks just because I didn't quite know what to say."

Cal thought he had known exactly what she was saying. She was just more interested in her research than she had ever been in being with him, but he wouldn't confide that point of view to her. Better to forget the whole thing and move on.

"It's okay—"

"No it isn't!" she insisted, seizing his arm and his ability to think rationally along with it.

For a brief moment, when all he could envision was climbing into her sweet embrace again, he wondered if he could forget about her crazy quest for information on mating rituals and take her out on a real date.

But that was an invitation to trouble. A surefire way to hurt each other and to disrupt the sane home life he planned to create for Allison.

"You don't understand, Cal. My life is inseparable from my work—wonderfully so, as far as I'm concerned. But I know other people find it annoying. I can't help but see how the whole world interacts on a sociological basis, even when I'm having the time of my life." She paused, biting her lip. "Well maybe not *while* I'm having the time of my life, but shortly thereafter."

He took her by the shoulders, needing to squelch her revelations before he started to really think about what she was saying. It would probably be better for all parties concerned if they distanced themselves a little bit.

"Honestly, Maddy, it wasn't a big deal."

She stiffened like vinyl seats in winter. "Excuse me, Cal, but it was a very big deal to me."

Ouch. In getting his nose out of joint about the whole thing, he had almost forgotten about it being her first time and all.

"Sorry." He released her shoulders and stepped back, wishing it could be that easy to let her go in his thoughts. "Are you okay?"

She stamped a foot, sending her long skirt in a fluttery little dance around her ankles. "Of course I'm okay. I just want you to hear my apology."

"You're still apologizing?"

"I'm still explaining it."

"I see."

He waited for her to continue, seeing no way to escape the conversation until Allison returned. But instead of proceeding with the scientific rationalization for her behavior, Madeline stared beyond him to a point on the horseshoe driveway.

Hearing a car door slam, Cal turned. He grinned

when he spied an older man paying a cabdriver. "Well, that's definitely not Allison."

Madeline still squinted at the man. "Nope. That's definitely the renowned physics professor, Dr. Watson. Looks like the real scientist has come to town, after all."

Maddy's father?

Great. Just what he needed—an irate father ready to dissect his guts for stealing Maddy's innocence against a car wash wall.

10

AFTER LEAVING MADELINE to her own devices in Louis-ville for five years, her father had to show up now? For a moment she almost considered ducking behind Cal and letting her dad find his way to her office—or wher-ever he was headed—on his own.

But she couldn't do that. As frustrating as he could be at times, Dr. Richard Watson had still raised Made-line single-handedly and had never in all that time ut-tered a bad word about the woman who had deserted them both. He deserved a warm welcome.

"Daddy!" she called, weaving around Cal to greet her father.

He looked older than he had at Christmas last year. More gray peppered his fair hair and his clothes hung loosely over his slight frame. His glasses were still twice as thick as hers, however, a badge of honor for the academic crowd.

Glancing up at Madeline, her father picked up his one garment bag and closed the distance between them. "Surprise, surprise, daughter! Fancy seeing my little scholar out here in the sunlight! I figured I would find you tucked away in some cavernous library, hip-deep in books and plotting your next research article."

No doubt that's where he thought she belonged. All

the same, affection unfurled for the man who'd done his best to bring up his only child.

She took his bag out of his hands, then hugged and kissed him. "I do try to have a life outside of work, Daddy."

Recalling the dynamic man who had dominated her life outside of work lately, Madeline turned to Cal.

He stood with arms crossed, peering out at the street, probably hoping his sister would return before Madeline dragged him into conversation.

"Cal?" For some reason, she wanted him to meet her father. Even when she and Cal had been just friends, he'd been more important to her than anyone else in town. She only hoped her father behaved. "I'd like you to meet my father, Dr. Richard Watson."

Cal took a wary step forward and offered his hand. "Cal Turner. Nice to meet you."

Madeline waited for her father to exercise a small amount of decorum—a hint of the civility he usually reserved for his physics cronies. Instead she watched him go into frost mode and hoped she hadn't just made a big mistake.

"How do you do?" Her father shook Cal's hand and then motioned to Maddy to come close.

How embarrassing. She smiled at Cal and dutifully leaned toward her dad.

He covered his mouth with one hand and stage whispered into her ear. "This isn't the man you were carrying on with last weekend, I hope."

Madeline recalled their conversation earlier in the week, in which her father had confronted her with the surveillance report of her activities with Cal. She glared at her father, squelching the urge to fling her arms around Cal to defend him. "I thought you'd enjoy meeting him precisely because he *is* the man I've been carrying on with, Daddy."

She heard Cal succumb to a sudden coughing fit, but never took her gaze from her father.

He raised a censorious brow. "I would think your studies would keep you too busy for that sort of thing, Madeline."

Forcing her lips into what she hoped was a polite smile, Madeline was about to ask her father if he'd like a tour around campus when he suddenly turned to Cal.

"Are you a 'social' scientist, too, young man?" Her father said it as if he feared the condition could be catching.

Madeline's mortification drowned along with Cal's reply in the resounding honk of a car horn.

Allison approached in her new white Chevrolet, waving through the window as she slid into a parking space. She jumped out, blond braids bouncing, oblivious to the undercurrents of the threesome standing curbside.

"It drives like a dream, Cal!" she called.

She flung herself around her brother in a gesture of unadulterated affection that no one had ever bestowed upon Madeline. Much as Madeline loved her dad, she would have gladly traded him in for Allison at the moment.

Madeline cleared her throat, prepared to slog her way through another introduction, but Allison plowed forward before Madeline had a chance.

"There was a little whirring sound when I drove it, though, Cal." She turned to hover over the car's hood. "Could you look at it just to be sure it's okay?"

"Gladly." Cal practically skipped over to the car. He looked ready to dissemble the engine screw by screw to escape the scarcely veiled hostility of Richard Watson.

Not that Madeline blamed him.

"My word," her father exclaimed, his eyes widening as Cal propped the hood and dove into the engine up to his elbows. "He fixes cars?"

Allison beamed. "He's a mechanic," she informed him with pride. "He once took an engine apart and put it back together blindfolded."

Her father whipped the handkerchief from his pocket and started mopping his forehead. "Well, perhaps we should allow him some space to work." He turned away from Cal and the automobile, ready to ignore Cal and the fact that Madeline had claimed him as her friend.

No wonder she'd never had any friends growing up. Her father was even more of an academic snob than she'd remembered.

He inclined his head toward Madeline. "So, daughter, I won't insult you by mincing words."

A sickening feeling in the pit of her stomach made her want to run. When had her father ever minced words?

"After I received that phone call notifying me that you were cavorting around campus in a questionable red dress, I heard some rumors that your dissertation has been turned down." He glared at her meaningfully. "So I had to come down here to see for myself what's going on. I've really got to wonder what has gotten into you all of the sudden."

Cal coughed, loudly, from under the hood.

Before Madeline could respond, Allison leaned in between them and hooked arms with Dr. Watson. "Madeline and I have each decided to get a life." Allison giggled, her grin a permanent fixture since she'd received her present.

Her father stared at Allison as if unsure how to react to her natural gregariousness. He probably hadn't exchanged this much non-physics-related conversation in one day since Madeline had left home. He might be a brilliant scientist and a member of the academic elite, but he still possessed the social skills of a middle school science nerd.

Before Madeline could think of a polite way to excuse them, Allison dashed back to her new car to check on Cal's progress.

Madeline stuffed her father's handkerchief back into his pocket for him, determined not to make a scene. "Why don't you go over to the science building, Daddy, and I can meet you there later? You must be exhausted from your trip."

He shook off her hand. "Honestly, Madeline, you treat me like I'm two steps from the nursing home. I only want what's best for my little girl." He smiled at her affectionately. "Can I help it if I take some fatherly pride in what you do?"

Cal slammed down the hood of Allison's car. "We're taking off now," he called while Allison waved. "Nice meeting you, Dr. Watson."

Relief pounded through Madeline. She just hoped Cal wasn't already seething at her father's rudeness. Now she could have a heart-to-heart with her father and put an end to his illusions of her settling down with a "real" scientist.

She waved back at Cal and his sister, hoping the awkwardness of her father's visit hadn't alienated Cal even more. "Have a good time," she called, stifling her regret that she wouldn't be spending the next hour with Cal, after all.

Dr. Watson managed a stiff nod, but Allison and Cal had already hopped in the car. They drove out of sight, leaving Madeline to figure out how to confront her father with the news she hadn't been able to break to him four years ago.

She didn't want to make the same choices—or mistakes—he had.

"Daddy, you really don't need to worry about me and Cal. We aren't going to get serious about each other right now, because we both have a lot of other things to accomplish." Such as her doctorate. Such as his guardianship of Allison.

She refused to think about what would happen after the custody hearing. Cal might defeat Aunt Delia's motion and win Allison, but Madeline knew he wouldn't suddenly decide to strike up a relationship with her. True to his bad boy ways, Cal obviously avoided seriously relationships like the plague.

Her father patted her shoulder in an awkward display of affection, then pulled away again. Maddy appreciated the tiny offering, knowing it had always been difficult for her father to be demonstrative. And he only grumbled because he wanted to protect her.

He lowered his voice. "It's just that I'm hearing wild reports about you, honey, and I'm worried it might be someone else's influence distracting you from your goals." He tugged at the collar of his button-down.

No doubt the warm Kentucky afternoon was a far cry from upstate New York this time of year.

She patted his shoulder, mirroring the small gesture he'd made. "No one is going to distract me, Dad." Not even a certain hunky business teacher, she promised herself.

"Yet you compromised your standing in front of your university peers by allowing yourself to be carried around the parking lot last weekend like a sack of potatoes."

"No one is going to think any less of me for something so innocent, Dad." She smiled, hoping to lighten the tension between them.

He stared back at her, expressionless.

"Unless you do, that is." She half feared his response. She'd been worried about living up to this man's expectations all her life, and no matter how much trouble he caused, she couldn't help but want to please him.

"Of course not," he mumbled, looking distinctly uncomfortable at her direct approach. "I just don't know that an outsider like your mechanic would be able to appreciate the finer points of university politics. He might not have realized what he did was wrong." He flashed her a kind smile to make up for his elitist words.

Okay, enough was enough. She loved her dad to no end and she owed him all the world, but he was pushing her every last button with this discussion. "Cal knows plenty about university politics, Dad, because he teaches here, too. And he only carried me to his car to prevent me from parading around campus in the most shocking red dress you've ever seen. He probably did you a favor with that move."

Her father frowned, turning his lip outward like a petulant child. "Why didn't he mention being a professor?"

She sighed. Much as she didn't want to have an unpleasant conversation with her dad, she didn't see a choice now. She should have stood up to him long ago.

Taking a deep breath, she looked at him levelly. "Maybe Cal doesn't feel the need to validate himself by announcing his academic credentials every time he meets someone."

She left it unsaid that her father demanded to be introduced as "doctor." She also left it unsaid that Cal's comfort in his own skin appealed to her more than any other part of his gorgeous self.

Her father stroked his shaven jaw, mirroring the stance of *The Thinker* behind him. "Shouldn't he be proud of his accomplishments?"

"I think he's just proud of his other accomplishments, too," Madeline replied, grasping for the first time how humble Cal had always been, despite his thriving business and the degree on his wall. "He's raising his sister in the aftermath of his father's death. He has started a chain of successful garages. He cares about his pass/fail average every semester...."

Madeline slowed herself down, realizing she'd reeled off an awful lot of things to like about Cal. Still, she couldn't resist revealing one final bit of information to change her father's mind about Cal.

"Best of all, Daddy, Cal is the rare kind of guy who can fully appreciate a 283-cubic-inch engine that produces 270 horses in a classic car. He can't be that bad, can he?"

Birds chirped a cheerful response to her question, but the good doctor remained silent.

Madeline had played her trump card with the horse-power remark. If that failed to impress her father, she couldn't imagine what would.

"He teaches here?" he finally asked.

She nodded, hopeful.

Her father fanned himself with his hand, looking thoughtful. "And he shares our interest in classic automobiles?"

A smile itched Madeline's lips. Her father might have been his usual ill-mannered self today, but he'd meant well. He'd only been looking out for her, after all. "He's got a fifty-seven Chevy that's pristine navy blue, and sweet enough to eat, Daddy. He probably would have shown it to you if you'd been nicer to him."

Dr. Watson couldn't have looked more deflated than if he'd just lost his research grant. "Why didn't you tell me before?"

She shrugged, then ventured a consoling arm across his tweed-covered shoulders. They might not see eye-to-eye on how to pursue an academic career, but Madeline and her father had always enjoyed the common ground of their love of old cars. Some of her most pleasant memories as a child had been the days she'd coerced her father into attending a car show. They would ride deep into the countryside to join the other car hounds, peering through windshields and under hoods.

He brightened. "Maybe I ought to get to know this young man of yours a little better."

Madeline could see the wheels turning in her father's brilliant mind. The last thing she needed was for him to seek out Cal. "He's awfully busy with his work," she assured him.

"What man is too busy to talk about the woman in his life?" He straightened his jacket and retrieved his bag. "Don't worry, sweetheart, I'm sure I'll find time to have a man-to-man talk with him at some point this weekend."

Great. Her fit of temper had backfired.

Madeline could just see it. Her five-and-a-half-foot father telling six-foot Cal to behave himself in one breath, and in the next trying to wheedle a ride in the antique car.

Her father would have Cal running in the opposite direction in no time.

And as much as she might tell herself that she and Cal were better off apart anyway, the thought of Cal missing from her life threatened to leave a gaping, empty space inside her.

Just about the size of her heart.

CAL USUALLY ENJOYED spending Saturdays working on his cars. Today, however, as he pulled open the doors of the barn he'd converted into a garage, he couldn't scavenge much enthusiasm for his favorite hobby. His head still spun from his talk with Maddy and his first meeting with Dr. Richard Watson.

It had been evident from the man's pinched frown that he wished Cal would crawl back under a rock and leave Madeline alone.

Instead, Cal crawled under the white Thunderbird with his rubber mallet, prepared to knock out the worst of the dent Allison had given it the other night. He went to work with gentle taps, thinking that his encounter with Dr. Watson should have reminded Cal of all the reasons he ought to stay away from Maddy.

They both taught at U of L, but before that, they had obviously come from two different planets. They were headed in different career directions, too.

Cal taught because he liked to share his knowledge and maybe to save a few people the hard knocks that he'd taken in the business world. But teaching could only be a secondary job for him. His first interest would always be his business.

Madeline taught because she belonged to the academic elite, like her father. One day she'd publish her papers in fancy journals and tour the country on long sabbaticals, spending semesters as a guest lecturer at the universities of her choice.

Their paths probably wouldn't cross too much in the future. And Maddy had already made it clear she didn't want a relationship in her life right now.

So why waste time thinking about her nonstop?

He hit his thumb with the mallet and swore. He had

to get his head on straight soon, preferably before he lost a finger to his absentmindedness.

Maybe he'd settle down tonight with a trip to the library. He'd been meaning to check out a few books on the psychology of teenage wunderkinds. His sister deserved a well-informed brother, at least.

"Excuse me?" a voice called from somewhere outside Cal's backyard-barn-turned-garage. "Cal Turner?"

Cal figured only a salesperson would be out here on a Saturday asking for him by his full name. He debated pretending he wasn't home.

Whoever it was entered the garage, judging by the click of shoes against the concrete floor.

Apparently this person wasn't going to give up easily.

The intruder let out a long, low whistle.

Either a gorgeous woman had somehow materialized in Cal's converted garage for the intruder to admire, or the newcomer had an eye for cars.

Hoping to take his mind off Madeline for a few minutes, Cal pulled himself out from under the front fender.

And came face-to-face with the pinched-frown father of the woman who dominated his dreams. Only now the good professor wasn't wearing the pinched frown. No, Dr. Richard Watson's mouth currently hung wide open as his eyes ran appreciatively over the lines of Cal's fifty-eight Thunderbird.

Cal propped himself up against one of the barn's inner support beams and watched as Maddy's tweed-clad father all but drooled over the biggest prize in Cal's car collection.

Cal couldn't take his usual pride in showing off his automotive gem, however. Not when he knew Dr. Watson had probably spent the last two days telling Maddy all the reasons why Cal wasn't fit to so much as carry her books home from school.

"Can I help you?" Cal said finally.

Dr. Watson nodded vaguely, still staring at the car. "Madeline said you had a fifty-seven Chevy, but she never mentioned a thing about this." He gestured at the T-bird.

"She hasn't seen it." Cal didn't take this car out very often. She wouldn't see it unless she came to his house.

The idea held a disturbing amount of appeal.

Damn, but he had to get her and her crazy dissertation project out of his mind.

Dr. Watson smiled. "She would be impressed."

Cal didn't want to think about impressing Maddy. Better that he left her alone. He waited, knowing Maddy's father hadn't come here to talk about cars.

"She's a good girl, you know," the professor said at last, turning to face Cal. "Just a little unfocused at times. She's always been a bit too scattered to really discipline herself."

Cal struggled to follow the conversation. "Are we talking about your daughter?"

Dr. Watson stiffened. "Of course."

"Maddy is the most disciplined woman I've ever met."

Her father smiled indulgently. "That may be, son,

but in her field she needs to work more rigorously than in other professions."

Cal had the feeling Dr. Watson saw little self-discipline involved in the life of a car mechanic. "I'm sure she knows what she's doing," he replied.

Or at least she knew what she was doing in her work life, Cal silently amended. He couldn't help but wonder if she regretted her recent decisions in her personal life.

"Nevertheless," her father continued evenly, "I wanted to come out here to ask your support in helping her achieve her career goals."

In other words, stay the hell away from my daughter. Cal read the message loud and clear.

"She told me you are one of her closest friends," the professor continued, "so I know you will want to help her as much as I do."

Her closest friend.

Thank God the professor didn't know how close they'd recently become. Cal shut out a tantalizing image of Maddy covered in pink soap bubbles.

Cal took a stabilizing breath. "I want her to be happy, sir."

Dr. Watson smiled. "Good. My Madeline is a sharp girl and she'll go as far as she wants to if she sets her mind to it."

"Maddy is the smartest woman I know," Cal agreed.

The man actually rose up on his toes. Her father beamed. "I can see we share more than one common interest then." He peered around the converted barn. "Would you mind showing me the Chevy before I leave you to your peace?"

The professor looked so genuinely hopeful, Cal didn't have a choice. But as he led the way to the smaller shed that held the Chevy, Cal had the feeling that he'd just agreed to more than an automotive demo.

He'd made a tacit agreement with the professor to keep his hands off Madeline. Something he wondered if he'd be able to do. Maybe if Maddy continued on her quest to trash her reputation and tumble headlong into trouble every chance she got, he would be able to keep his distance.

After all, what had drawn him to her from the beginning had been her oh-so-proper respectability and her unbelievable smarts. Although the short skirts had definitely made him a little crazy, they weren't what Madeline Watson was really about.

He needed to at least lay low until after the guardianship hearing had passed. He hadn't caused too much of a scene with Madeline yet, but there was still another week until the hearing for him to mess up. Heaven knew, between her stilettos and her steely determination to explore her untamed side, Madeline sizzled like an overheated radiator waiting to explode.

Cal still really wanted the sizzle.

But this was one time in his life he couldn't afford to get burned.

11

MADELINE TREKKED across campus, her breath curling into white wisps in the chilly night air. She hitched the strap of her book bag a little higher on her shoulder to resettle the weight of her notepaper and books. What a way to spend a Saturday.

Banners reading *Go Cardinals* hung from every archway. The brick academic halls bore bright red and yellow team spirit signs. Someone had stamped oversize cardinal footprints with yellow paint on the sidewalk from the parking lot to the library.

The rest of the student body seemed to have deserted the school grounds for the football game at Cardinal Stadium. Even her father had caught Cardinal fever, attending the game with his physics buddy.

Her dad seemed to be having the time of his life this trip, despite the insufficient size of the local physics conference. Today he'd made it a point to visit Cal and apparently had wheedled his way into seeing Cal's car collection.

Madeline couldn't help but feel a little left out. She envied the hours her father had spent with Cal, time she'd once taken for granted when Cal had been her friend.

She'd missed him this week. She hardly counted their confrontational encounter on Thursday as time spent together. What would it be like after Allison's guardianship hearing? Would Cal have any time left for Madeline, or would he be glad for an excuse to put space between them?

Trudging up the few steps to Ekstrom Library, Madeline consoled herself that at least she'd learned a lesson from what had happened with Cal. She knew now that she'd gone about her dissertation project all wrong. Cal had told her she shouldn't try to change her reputation or alter her image to sway the review committee, and he'd been right.

If she had been thinking rationally, she would have capitalized on her strengths as Cal had suggested instead of rushing to the mall to buy the slinkiest dress in stock. She needed to go back to the books and to develop a dynamite project proposal to convince even her most skeptic detractor that respectable Madeline Watson knew what she was doing.

Tugging open the library door, Madeline stepped back into comfortable terrain—the cavernous world of periodicals and microfiche. She dropped off her books to return at the main desk and made a beeline for the wide staircase. The library closed early on Saturdays, so she needed to make an efficient sweep for materials and then head over to the Honors building to review them at her leisure.

She had already hit the first step when she experienced the irresistible urge to turn around. A sixth sense called her backward, halting her in midstride. Her other five senses leaped into hyper-drive, sending a shiver of awareness through her.

Madeline followed her instincts and pivoted, knowing who she would see before she actually spied him. Cal sat on a bench about twenty feet away, absorbed in a book and oblivious to her presence.

Savoring the moment, Madeline allowed herself the pure pleasure of looking at him. He hadn't bothered with a collared shirt or khakis tonight. He'd opted for his most comfortable clothes to work in the library. Clad in jeans and a blue T-shirt with the Perfect Timing logo, he looked better than most men could manage in a tuxedo.

Soft cotton stretched and hugged wide shoulders. He leaned forward, elbows on his knees, holding his book out in front of him. His hazel eyes darted efficiently across the page, all his attention focused on the hardback volume bearing the title *Parenting the Precocious Child.*

Ouch. Madeline took a deep breath and told herself to be grateful for the clear reminder that Cal had other things on his mind right now. He couldn't afford to embroil himself in her crazy stunts. And he definitely didn't want a repeat performance of the other night, much as she might wish otherwise.

She'd be wise to walk away, to leave Cal alone to fight his battle for Allison without her in the way.

Gulping in one last delicious look at him, Madeline sighed. It wouldn't be easy to do the right thing, but if she ever wanted to salvage a friendship with Cal, she'd have to find a way to quench the acute case of lust she seemed to have developed for him.

"Maddy?" Cal's voice rolled over her, capturing her in a net of her own desires once again.

Part of her wanted to stamp her foot in frustration,

while the other part wanted to pump her fist in the air and shout a triumphant, "Yes!"

She spun to face him, but didn't make a move to get closer. "Hey, Cal."

He snapped his book shut and rose. Closing the distance between them with his usual lazy grace, he eyed her carefully. "You weren't going to just disappear upstairs without saying hi, were you?"

She shrugged. "I thought I'd better leave you alone until the whole guardianship thing dies down."

Seeing the grave look on his face, she couldn't hold back a smile to share with him. "You'll do a great job with Allison, Cal. You already do."

Cal shook his head. "I don't know, Maddy. She went to the football game tonight with her friends."

Madeline laughed, grateful for a topic to focus on besides their relationship. "No wonder you're hiding out in the library."

"I'll just stare at the clock if I'm home."

It flittered on the tip of her tongue to tell him he just needed something more engaging to think about to make the time pass faster, but she wouldn't. Not anymore.

Her days of fierce flirtation with Cal were over.

She drifted up another step and readjusted her book bag on her shoulder. "Well, good luck distracting yourself. Guess I'll go get to work on my research."

Cal followed her up a step. "Research?"

He touched her arm lightly for all of a second. Madeline felt the stab of hunger straight down to her toes.

Clearing his throat, he folded his arms resolutely over his chest. "What are you working on?"

The question caught her by surprise, but not half as much as Cal's seeming reluctance to let her go. "I'm following your suggestion, actually, and going back to the drawing board on my dissertation proposal. I thought I'd gather some more source material before the library closes."

A group of students brushed past them on their way up the stairs, and Madeline found herself gently protected by Cal's hand curved around her elbow.

She backed up another step, and out of his reach, unwilling to subject herself to the temptation of his touch.

Cal didn't seem to notice. He grinned at her instead. "You're not going to find a man to parade around campus?"

His grin was infectious, and she could already feel an answering smile twitch at her lips.

"No."

His eyes narrowed. "And you're not going to paint the town in red silk and stilettos anymore?"

She shook her head. "Not too often, anyway."

He took two steps up the stairs, putting them at eye level. "You're actually going to hang on to your pristine reputation and follow *my* advice?"

Madeline could feel the heat of his nearness, smell the clean scent of his laundry detergent. In a flash of vivid memory, she thought of them entwined at his car wash, slick with water and soap, sliding against each other in a hungry search for completion.

Nodding, she gripped his shoulders and edged him backward to insert some space between them. "Yes, Cal, it was good advice, and maybe I should have listened to you all along. But I can't say I regret what happened between us." She shoved her hands into her pockets to keep her from doing something foolish like touching him again.

His tawny eyebrows lifted in unison. "You don't?"

She thought about herself in her skyscraper heels. She'd almost broken her neck a few times, of course. And she'd never made such a spectacle of herself as she had in her black leather skirt. But there could be no denying.

She'd loved every minute of her adventure.

"Not a chance."

He reached for her hand and pulled her down the stairs, past the reference section, to the back of the library.

Madeline walked double time to keep up.

Steering her to a pair of chairs in the corner, he sat in one and tugged her down into the other. When they were safe from any nearby ears, he leaned close and whispered. "Then why are you running away?"

Her heart jumped in reaction to his proximity. She wanted nothing more than to lean into him, to toss her book bag on the floor and slide onto his lap. But she couldn't.

"You know why...bad timing, a guardianship hearing, my father in town...shall I go on?"

"In another week, all that disappears. What then?"

She hadn't really wanted to confront that particular issue. But she knew the answer. "Then you have Allison to focus on while I have a doctorate to pursue and a dissertation to write."

"No place for a mechanic in the life of a Ph.D. candidate?'' The edge in his voice no doubt came from the rude way her father had treated him.

She shook her head. "That's not it and you know it."

"Then explain it to me." His hazel eyes probed hers with an intensity that unsettled her. "What's to stop us from exploring this thing between us once Allison's future is secure? What if we can figure out a way to protect her from any...repercussions...of our relationship?"

Madeline shook her head. "Allison's too smart to be kept in the dark for long, and you wouldn't want to shut her out like that, anyway." She knew how much Cal loved his sister, how much he wanted to protect her from an unstable home life. Madeline had the impression his marriage had been one hell of a rocky ride, even though he didn't like to talk about it. "Besides, the university doesn't approve of relationships between grad students and teachers." They both needed to remember that.

She'd been prepared for a quick fling with Cal—one that would capture attention and be over with it before it really began. But the administration could give them grief if they started seeing each other on a regular basis.

"What can they say, Maddy? You're closer to being faculty than I am. And our roots go deeper than U of L. We've known each other four years and two months, remember?"

She remembered, all right. She remembered so well that she'd committed the reasons she couldn't be with him to memory.

"Then there's the lack of time," she continued. "The

doctoral program is all-consuming, especially with me teaching, too," she said. "And I don't want to just skate through to get a Ph.D. I want to do research that is publishable, and to make a significant contribution to the field. I can't do that and do justice to a relationship, too."

"So you're just willing to give up on us without even trying?"

"I did try, Cal! And I ended up hurting you because I have sociology on the brain and said something stupid."

He grinned. "I think you were just nervous because the earth moved."

She silently thanked him for the levity. She hated for there to be tension between them. "Maybe so. I hope that means I'm forgiven."

Cal waved an impatient hand through the air. "I realize it was selfish of me to get my nose out of joint about something so insignificant when you had just committed something precious to me."

He couldn't have touched her heart more if he had just handed her a Hallmark card. Little happy tears itched the backs of her eyes. She wouldn't dare shed one right now, not when she needed to convince Cal things wouldn't work between them.

He would demand so much more of her—deserve so much more of her—than she could afford to give during the next few years. She couldn't bear to hurt him the same way her father had unwittingly alienated her mother.

The hushed quiet of the library seemed suddenly intimate instead of comforting. The silence magnified the clicking of computer keys across the room.

She nodded, her motions feeling jerky and uncoordinated. "I considered that night an equal exchange. Your gift to me was pretty, um, good, too."

Cal's gaze dipped below her face to slide over her body for the briefest of instants.

Madeline ignored the urge to follow suit.

He sucked in a deep breath. "We'd better change the subject before—"

"By all means." The mere thought of that night wreaked havoc on her vital signs, and she needed to keep her wits about her if she was going to accomplish her study mission here tonight. "So do you think we can go back to the sort of friendship we used to have?"

Cal blinked. "Go back?"

Isn't that what they'd been talking about? Hadn't Madeline made it clear she would only disappoint him if she tried to give him anything more? She nodded. "To being friends."

Cal wondered if his head reeled because he'd been inhaling too deeply in the quest for a whiff of Maddy's raspberry scent, or if it was because she'd truly just offered him the very thing he'd thought he wanted.

Just friendship.

"Platonic friends?" Her father would turn cartwheels at the idea. But it didn't sound like quite enough anymore.

She smiled that patient teacher smile that made him feel like the smartest kid in class. Too bad he knew otherwise.

Platonic friendship suddenly sounded like a prison

sentence. As much as he had thought that would be better for her, now he didn't know if he could be satisfied with something so tame. "I don't know if we can ever really go back to the way we were, Maddy."

He was sorry he'd said it when her shoulders slumped. Even her book bag strap fell off one arm.

Damn.

He plowed forward, needing to explain himself, hoping she'd understand. "I just don't see how it would work when I'm fighting myself to not touch you right now."

She stood abruptly, almost knocking the library chair over in her wake. "Then we'd better go back to my initial plan for today, Cal. We avoid each other." She didn't sound mad exactly, but Cal noticed her hands shook just a little.

A few heads turned in their direction.

Cal glanced around them and lowered his voice another notch. "Because you don't have time for me?"

Madeline lifted her pointed chin, tilting the precariously balanced knot of her hair to one side of her head. "No." She paused. "Maybe. But it sounds so awful when you say it like that. It's more that we both can't afford a relationship right now. And we definitely can't afford to make a scene for the next week, though we seem destined to create one."

Cal rose, but she'd already backed away.

"I'm just going to head upstairs now and do my work." She pointed over her shoulder, her voice wobbling with whatever emotions she fought to hide. "Why don't you go back to reading your book and being friends with other, less theatrical females?" She turned and hurried away, taking the stairs two at a time until she disappeared from sight.

What the hell was that all about?

Cal raked a hand through his hair and wondered how other men managed to understand women.

She was mad at *him* for wanting more? She had tested him to the limits of his endurance with her provocative outfits, her warm honey kisses and her entreaties to teach her something of the mating ritual, yet she had the nerve to rail at him for needing her?

Cal hadn't wanted to need her. He'd told her father just this afternoon that he thought he could help her in her career goals and stay away from her.

And he'd tried. When he'd seen her tonight, he hadn't wanted to call to her. In fact, his feet had walked over to her on their own volition.

But she'd stirred a longing in him that hadn't come close to being quenched.

Oh, no. Madeline Watson couldn't blithely return to the safety of their platonic friendship after offering him a glimpse of her uninhibited self. And, lucky for him, she had taught him exactly how to seduce the object of his desire.

How would the Lady Scholar feel when the tables were turned? When he was the one teasing her to a frenzy, tempting her with what she wanted more than her damn Ph.D.?

Would she be so quick to say she didn't have time for him then?

Cal intended to find out. Because as long as they weren't flaunting an affair in public, there wasn't anything wrong with him pursuing Madeline Watson.

No matter what she said about the administration's disapproval, Cal knew he was too small a fish for the university to worry about. He wasn't a faculty member, and Madeline wasn't his student. Even her father couldn't object as long as they were discreet and Maddy put enough time into her studies.

Cal wasn't about to wait another week to find out if she was serious about returning to a platonic relationship. He would begin his sensual onslaught as soon as Maddy's father left town.

Thanks to his long visit with Dr. Watson over the hood of the Chevy, Cal knew the professor flew out at nine in the morning. Which meant he'd be ringing Madeline's doorbell with brunch by eleven.

Smiling as he considered the erotic possibilities of pancake syrup, Cal knew he'd found the perfect middle ground with Maddy. They could be together as long as they kept things simple...and discreet.

AFTER ONE LAST WAVE to her father's departing taxi, Madeline wandered back into the house and collapsed on the overstuffed sofa, sending a surge of throw pillows to the floor. She'd enjoyed seeing him, but she was exhausted from the emotional drain of the weekend. Between worrying about her dissertation, her father showing up unexpectedly, and Cal...

Well, she wouldn't think about Cal. But if she had been thinking about him, she'd surely be exhausted from wondering how to treat their strange new relationship.

What did he expect to happen now? He'd squashed her hope that they could go back to being friends. And she knew he didn't want a serious relationship in his life any more than she did. At least, she didn't think so.

She knew very little about his divorce, but she knew it had hurt him enough that he didn't want to tread down the aisle again anytime soon. And, in the four years that she'd known him, he'd never had a serious girlfriend.

So where did that leave her? He didn't want to be just friends, and they were both too gun-shy for a committed relationship. Did he plan to just walk away? Pretend their good rapport and scintillating sex had never happened?

She considered calling him to inform him how ridiculous that was, but she needed to get busy on her research work today. Hauling herself off the couch, she vowed she would stick to her ritual of making Sundays serious reading days.

Rose Marie had left a message on Friday to say she might have some good news pertaining to Madeline's dissertation review by today, but Madeline wasn't going to count on that. As much as she hoped Rose Marie would have something valuable to offer, Madeline knew she was ultimately responsible for her own work. And that meant burying herself in periodicals today.

As she pulled out a new stack of bound magazines from under the dining room table, Madeline's doorbell rang.

Why did she only get visitors when her house was a wreck? Walking to the door, she caught a glimpse of a white Chevy in her front driveway. Allison's car.

But the way her pulse pounded her flesh, she had a

premonition—or was it wishful thinking?—that it wouldn't be Allison on her doorstep.

She peered through the peephole, but all she could see were grocery bags.

"Hey, gorgeous, it's me." The supermarket sacks muffled the voice, but that sexy low rumble could only belong to one man.

Madeline wished she weren't wearing an old T-shirt and pajama bottoms, but she refused to let her limited vanity come between her and curiosity. She opened the door wide and stood out of the way.

Cal swayed with his mountain of packages, then crossed the threshold to her dining room table, trailing the scent of fresh fruit and crisp morning air behind him.

Rubbing her arms to warm herself, she shivered—a reaction not entirely due to the chill breeze. She shut the door and followed him, all the while admonishing herself to stop being so ridiculously happy to see him.

He didn't want anything to do with her anymore, did he?

Her belly growled in hungry approval of the citrus scents. "*Mmm.* Is that pineapple I smell?"

He grinned as he dropped the armload of food on the table. "Good morning to you, too."

The words reminded her of a simple intimacy she wouldn't be able to share with this man. She'd never wake up to see his face beside her on a pillow.

She cleared her throat to frame a response. "Good morning."

How had her greeting ended up sounding as sultry as a come-on line?

Flustered, she pointed to the bags on the table. "What's all this?"

"Breakfast in bed."

She experienced that "falling off the monkey bars" sensation again, a stunned breathlessness that only Cal Turner seemed to produce in her.

Once she could breathe again, she folded her arms across her chest. "Presumptuous of you, don't you think? I mean, yesterday you didn't think we could be so much as friends and today you think you can wheedle your way into my bed?"

He canted closer. "Who said anything about me being in your bed?" The gentle warmth of his voice belied his statement.

Madeline closed her eyes for a moment and saw Cal between her sheets, feeding her pineapple pieces with his teeth.

Had she been cold only a minute ago? Heat flooded her veins, suffused her flesh.

"At least," his voice drawled over her, "I wouldn't be in your bed without an explicit invitation. I'm just going to feed you."

Madeline's eyes fluttered open, and she realized he'd come closer, his body inches from hers.

She wanted to tip her head back and kiss him. She longed to press herself against his chest to see if he felt as heartachingly good as she remembered.

Instead, she forced her gaze back down at the table. "That looks like way too much breakfast for one person."

A slow smile spread over his face. "Darling, that sounds like an invitation if ever I've heard one."

12

MADELINE ABSORBED his words until they finally slid into place in her head.

Cal Turner *wanted* her.

Her mouth went dry, her jaw went slack, and her glasses started a slow slide down the bridge of her nose. She pushed them back into place, staving off an impulse to charge down the hall and tear through the closets for her sheath dress. She'd felt in control when dressed for seduction, when *she* was the one making the advances.

Without the armor of her temptress trappings, she felt more vulnerable to the deeper tug of attraction between them...the one that wasn't based just on physical attraction, but on soul-deep need.

Cal loomed next to her. His hands fell softly on her arms. "So what do you say, Maddy? Was that an invitation, or just my wishful thinking?"

The unspoken implication of spending the day burning up the sheets with him hung heavy in the air between them.

Could she ever let him go if she gave in to a day so intimate?

"I don't know, Cal. Maybe I'd better not—"

He stepped back from her immediately and held up his hand in mock surrender. "You'd rather have breakfast on the couch. Not a problem." He hustled over to the shopping bags and started hauling them into the kitchen. "You just make yourself at home, honey, and I'll treat you to the best omelet you've ever eaten."

Speechless at how fast the man could change direction, she watched him spread the makings for a feast on her counter.

No more than fifteen minutes later, the heady scent of ham and cheese wafted from the kitchen, while Elvis crooned from Cal's CD in her living room. Madeline sat with her feet propped on an ottoman, leafing through the copy of the *Courier Journal* Cal had brought along with him.

Her house had never seemed so homey and Madeline knew she was fast sinking into deep, deep trouble. If this kept up, she'd be falling head over heels for Cal, and then she'd never be satisfied with only his friendship. She had to put a stop to this.

Tossing the newspaper aside, she stood. "Cal?"

"No need to get up. I've got everything." He balanced two plates on his arms while carrying two glasses of orange juice. Utensils wrapped in napkins stuck out of his shirt pocket.

Madeline's belly growled again, firmly protesting her plan to ask him to leave. How could she refuse a guy who'd just cooked her breakfast? She hadn't been that spoiled since...well, ever. Her father understood everything about physics except at what temperature to cook food without burning it to a crisp.

She would allow herself this one indulgence. Then, after their omelets, she'd thank Cal politely and explain why they couldn't continue seeing each other on such awkward, nebulous terms. They needed to define their relationship and to stick to the parameters they set.

Her conscience appeased for a little while longer, Madeline soaked up the aromas and salivated over the plate Cal sat in front of her.

"This looks fabulous." She wondered what it would be like to be with Cal on a long-term basis. Had he cooked Sunday brunches for his wife? Hard to believe any woman would give up a man like Cal and omelets to boot.

"Allison is teaching me how to cook," he confessed as he took the wing-backed chair across from her. "I have to admit, it's pretty rewarding."

"I don't know the first thing about cooking. That kitchen is mostly a stockpile of the microwavable meals I live on." Madeline groaned at the first cheesy bite. "Your sister really is a genius."

Elvis tunes traded off with Sam Cooke and Bobby Darrin, surrounding them in fifties music. Madeline felt like the school nerd who'd captured the class rebel's attention at the sockhop.

"Why didn't I know that about you?" Cal asked between bites.

"That my cooking skills are nonexistent?"

"That you'd rather sustain yourself with cardboard dinners than ever go out?"

"I like going out," Madeline argued. "In fact, I only just learned that about myself. I had a really good time the other night."

She'd meant her trip to the cowboy bar, and her brief time pretending to be someone more brazen than herself. But of course, the moment she said it, she thought of that *other* night they'd gone out. And never made it any further than his workplace.

She felt his eyes linger on her, but she concentrated on sipping her orange juice. His knee grazed hers, reminding her of his proximity.

He set his fork down on his empty plate. "Then why don't we do it again?"

Desire swirled low in her belly. A hunger assailed her that wouldn't be squelched by another bite of omelet.

Heat clawed its way up her cheeks. She hadn't expected him to be so direct. "Well, I, um—"

"I mean, maybe if we went out together a few times, we could get a better handle on what's going on between us." Cal smiled innocently.

He pushed back his chair and began clearing their plates.

"Oh." Had she misunderstood? Or did that little grin mean he'd been playing with her?

She listened to him rattle around in the kitchen for a minute, incensed that he would tease her about what had happened between them. But then he came back with a tray laden with pineapple and oranges, strawberries, and—her favorite—raspberries. Cheese and bread sat in a little basket alongside the fruit.

She forgot all about her frustration to marvel over his decadence.

"You must have bought out the supermarket." She picked at a green grape hanging off one side of a crystal platter she'd owned for years and never used.

He placed the tray on the ottoman and then pulled

the wing-backed chair over beside the couch. "I had a hunch you'd been going without for too long."

She frowned. "You're teasing me today."

He reached over and took her shoulders in his hands. Gently, he leaned her back on the couch pillows. "I'm flirting with you, Maddy. You fast-forwarded on the mating ritual lessons so much that we skipped the flirting chapter."

"Oh." She couldn't seem to think clearly with him inclined over top of her.

Slowly, he eased away again, but only long enough to select a stout strawberry from the platter. He moved to sit next to her on the sofa, and brought the berry to her mouth. Touching the seeded skin to her lip, he tempted her with the scent.

He rolled the berry along her lower lip, his gaze riveted to her mouth. "But if you have time today, we could correct that omission with a few simple exercises."

A cold drop of juice rolled down her chin. Before she could reach to wipe it off, Cal bent over her and licked it away with his tongue.

The movement transpired so swiftly, she might have thought she'd fantasized it, if not for the way her flesh sizzled in that one, moist spot.

He held the berry above her mouth, his voice low and inviting in her ear. "What do you think, Maddy? Are you ready for a taste of what you missed out on last time?"

She wanted a taste so badly she couldn't see straight. Damn the consequences. She'd hated every last minute without him this week. Right now, all her nerve endings leaped to life, as if every last one of them reached and thirsted for Cal's touch.

She had already messed up their friendship with her determined efforts to seduce him. What could it hurt to indulge her desire for him just one more time?

Arching her neck, she lifted her head to the dangling fruit and snapped it from the stem with her teeth. Sweet juice burst over her tongue and seeped down her throat as she chewed.

Cal watched her like a starving man. To ensure he got the message, she licked her lips to seek out every last bit of liquid.

She cupped his cheek in her hand and tilted his gaze to her eyes. "I'm ready for more than a taste."

Cal about swallowed his tongue as he fought to continue breathing. For a woman who almost missed the double entendres he'd thrown her way earlier, Madeline Watson was a damn quick study.

He placed one finger over her lips and tossed a strawberry into his own mouth to quell his sudden thirst for the taste. "But this time, we're taking it slow. We're doing things my way."

She nipped his finger with her teeth to free her lips. "Just don't make me go without for too much longer."

Plucking up a pineapple piece, he slid the fruit into her mouth. "Honey, I'm going to indulge you like you've never been indulged before."

It unsettled him to realize how much he meant that statement. After seeing her sparse little kitchen with nothing but microwave meals, and knowing the way she denied herself the most simple pleasures in life, Cal wanted nothing more than to introduce her to a little excess. He wanted to feed her delicacies, wrap her in silk, and comb every inch of her waist-length hair with his fingers.

And that scared the hell out of him. He knew Maddy wasn't looking for a long-term relationship, and last he knew, neither was he. He refused to fail at another marriage, no matter how tempting the woman. But maybe if they kept things simple, they could both be happy. What would it hurt if they remained friends and...lovers?

He pulled the pen out of her hair that seemed to be holding the whole thing in a crooked knot. Brown silk uncoiled in a serpentine-like motion, then spread over the creamy colored couch pillows.

He forced himself to focus on her wide, dark eyes, and not her mouth. "Are you sure that's okay with you, Maddy? We can do things my way this time?"

A slow smile curled around the lips he was definitely not looking at. "Your way feels very promising to me."

He needed to be sure she understood. "But you're okay if we keep things just between us for a little longer, to protect Allison?"

"I'd never want to jeopardize your guardianship."

"You won't be offended if we lock the door and pull the curtains and hide from the world?"

"I'll feel flattered you want to keep me all to yourself."

Cal moved to bolt the door. "It won't be this way for long."

Sliding the lock into place, a thought flashed through his mind about what they'd do when they had to confront the outside world again. They couldn't stay locked in here forever. Still, he couldn't turn away from her now.

He returned to her side, grabbing a grape for each of them. "Thanks for understanding."

"I owe you, anyway." She scooted closer to sit hip to hip beside him. "Thanks for understanding my dad."

Her curves branded his side, scorching his flesh with her heat through the innocent brush of her soft cotton T-shirt.

"He didn't bother me." Cal fed her the grape, keenly aware of the contrast between the cool fruit and her warm lips as she accepted it from his fingers. "We ended up getting along okay."

"He means well, but he's pretty self-involved. It's hard for him to see beyond his science realm."

"Unlike his daughter, who forgets to ever think about herself." And unlike him, he amended silently, who could only seem to think about her.

She peered up at him, her eyes narrowed behind her glasses. "That's not true. I'm just as self-involved as my dad. It's a by-product of being a scholar."

He shook his head. "Just because you devote yourself to your work doesn't make you self-absorbed, Maddy. You always have time for other people—your students, Dr. Rose, my sister...me."

As the strains of "Blueberry Hill" drifted through the room, Cal knew the one kind of fruit he'd forgotten to get for Madeline. Still, he'd remembered the raspberries, the taste he'd been craving since his first date with her.

Reaching for a handful, he touched one to the hollow

of her throat and slid it down to the neck of her T-shirt. She shifted beside him, arching upward at his teasing touch.

He ate the skin-warmed berry off his finger and took another. Sweeping her fallen hair away from her ear, he bent over her to whisper, "You know, it's not really enough to eat one of these by itself."

"It's not?" She radiated heat like a warmed-up engine.

"I'd rather lick the taste off of you."

Her breathing hitched.

Slowly, he removed her glasses, careful to not pull any strands of hair along with them. She blinked as he set them on the end table. Then, he tugged her T-shirt off to expose the kind of white cotton bra he'd imagined her in long before the days of black lace and satin. He smiled to see it, gratified to think he'd known her so well, so intimately, all along.

Sliding off the seat and onto the floor in front of it, he pressed her back to recline across the couch. Her hair cradled her like a favored blanket, conforming to the slender length of her body.

He fought a primitive urge to tug her flannel pajama bottoms off, to feel her thighs around him again. But he'd given in to that hunger last time and regretted it. He wouldn't do it again. At least not until he'd awakened her senses and fired her need to burn as high and hot as his.

"Cal?" Her voice betrayed a hint of uncertainty.

He knew from experience her nervousness seemed to vanish when they touched. He grazed the soft plane of her belly with his fingertips, then squeezed a single raspberry over top of her navel. The juice filled the slight indentation, just trickling over both sides.

Cal bent his head to her midriff, taking in the clean, soapy scent of her. The only trace of raspberry fragrance rested in the dark pool at her waist.

Moving his lips over her taut flesh, he rejoiced in the small buck of her body when he inserted his tongue into her navel. Her hips curved up against his shoulder, her fingernails raked the creamy sofa upholstery.

Still, he took his time cleaning every drop of juice from her skin, trailing his tongue along the sides of her waist to the impediment of her pajama bottoms.

Madeline whimpered when he stopped there, wriggling her hips in unmistakable invitation.

Tugging the green flannel pants off her, he promised himself he would not rush. He was simply gaining more ground with which to tempt her.

Yeah, right. So he'd been dying to catch a glimpse of those thighs again. And maybe he'd been more than a little curious to see what his Lady Scholar wore for panties—white cotton with a little satin bow—but he was definitely taking his time.

Studiously ignoring the newly uncovered terrain, he leaned over to the ottoman to retrieve a chunk of pineapple with his teeth. He kept his hands pinned to the sides of the couch to prevent the greedy touches that would speed them along too soon.

Angling over her, he brought the fruit to rest against the slope of her breast. He slid the fruit downward, painting her skin in juice and gooseflesh as he went. At the thrust of her nipples through the white cotton of her bra, he reached to peel the straps from her shoulders, and unhooked the clasp in the front.

As more clothes disappeared from her body, Madeline wondered if anyone had ever hyperventilated during the mating ritual before.

Her senses swam as she stifled a gasp at Cal's provocative torment. He transferred the pineapple to one nipple and then the other before he ate it.

Desire lurched, sharp and edgy, inside her.

"Please," she whispered, seizing his shoulders. "I need you."

He paused to gaze into her eyes, seeing more deeply inside her soul than anyone had else had ever bothered to look. At that moment, Madeline knew they had gone too far.

This time would cost her so much more than before. The first time she'd lost her innocence. Now, her heart was in serious jeopardy. But she couldn't stop if she tried. Despite the threat of serious heartache, Madeline pulled Cal to her, needing the heavy press of his body on hers.

The new weight of his chest and thighs was deliciously familiar and foreign at the same time. His solid male form didn't give an inch, yet her body molded to accommodate his. His pineapple-raspberry breath worked faster than an aphrodisiac to heat her blood.

She reached for his shirt and dragged it over his back, off his body. The slide of his jeans against her bare thighs shifting her focus from her emotional needs to her physical hungers in a flash.

She didn't have a chance of running from this man. All she could do was stare up at him as he smoothed his palms down the length of her arms, then lifted her hands to rest over her head.

His lips moved down her neck to her breasts, nipping and tasting the flesh along the way. She only had to say no if she wanted to protect her heart from the inevitable break. All it would take was the slightest push of her hands against his broad shoulders.

But she couldn't find her voice, and her hands remained wantonly stretched over her head, where Cal had placed them. She wouldn't miss her chance to be cherished and adored, if only for a few hours.

Instead she centered all her attention on the play of his tongue over her skin, the slither of his hands along every inch of her body. When he had sampled every bit of her that was exposed, he grazed his stubbled cheek over the cotton fabric of her panties, igniting a soul-deep shiver within her.

He rained kisses along the waistband, and tugged at the satin bow with his teeth, until she wriggled impatiently beneath him. She wanted the satisfaction of completion, the fulfillment she'd experienced only once before, in the back-spray of Perfect Timing's car wash.

Yet even as he hitched one finger around the cotton fabric and pulled it down the length of her legs, he made no move to cover her with his body or to shed his own clothes.

He continued to administer lazy kisses along her hip where her panties had recently rested.

"Cal?" She grasped at his shoulders with her fingertips, desperate to hold him in her arms, inside her. Heat pooled between her legs, a swirling, restless ache.

He ignored her plea, sliding off the couch to kneel on the floor beside her. She whimpered her frustration until he settled one thigh over his shoulder and kissed her in the most shocking, delicious way.

"Cal," she gasped his name, then whispered, sighed and moaned it in turn as his tongue flicked over her again and again. The restless heat built until it shattered, pounding through her like a tidal wave to drown all her reservations, all her resistance.

But he gave no quarter, gently nipping the inside of her thigh. Immediately, the slow, warm swirl began all over again, tingling through her legs and breasts.

This time he cast off jeans and boxer shorts, pulling a condom from his pocket before he tossed aside his clothes. He covered her with his body and positioned himself between her legs.

He felt so good against her, so right. He combed his fingers through her hair and cradled her cheek with one hand, then eased his way inside her.

Madeline made the mistake of looking into his eyes at that moment, connecting with him on a level that went so much deeper than his body moving within her. Unable to sort out the tangle of feelings, she squeezed her thighs around him and reveled in the intense pleasure he wrought with every thrust of his hips.

He brought her unerringly to the brink she'd already hurtled over once. This time, he held her there, stretching out the dizzying feelings so that her release launched her even higher than before.

He trailed her by only a moment, his body surging with the force of his final surrender.

Madeline closed her eyes and wished she could remain there all day, shielded by his strong arms. But all too soon, the questions and uncertainties niggled at her.

Why was she relentlessly drawn to this man when she couldn't afford to have a relationship right now? Seeing her bachelor father this weekend reminded her of the difficulties involved in making a relationship work.

Despite her father's occasional surly disposition, he had tried his best when Madeline's mother had been around. Madeline knew her best wouldn't be good enough in the long run, either, especially for a guy like Cal who'd been burned once before. He wouldn't settle for any halfhearted commitment she might be able to make.

Then again, she didn't know if he would even be interested in any sort of commitment from her.

Sneaking a peek at the play of muscles across his chest, Madeline still couldn't believe the most notorious bad boy on campus had ever noticed someone like her.

"Cal?"

"Hmm?" He paused in the middle of kissing a tiny path from her chin to her ear.

"What ever made you notice me?" Maybe it was a dumb time to ask. But it was the kind of question she wouldn't have the nerve to confront him with another time.

His brow furrowed. "I've been noticing you for so long, it's hard to say."

She could almost be content with that answer.

Heaven knew, other men never noticed her at all unless she went to the trouble of body glitter and red silk. But she sensed from the way his eyes stared off into space that he was still considering the question.

She knew he had the answer when he smiled.

"You know, I'm going to have to answer this in two parts, because men don't always notice what they should about a woman." He pulled a long strand of hair out from in between them and laid it on the couch alongside her.

"First, I remember noticing one of those big shirts of yours and wondering what you kept all buttoned-up underneath it."

She rolled her eyes and gave him a reprimanding poke in the arm.

"Hey, I warned you. But you'll probably like that answer better than the second part."

Oh, great. Madeline hoped she wouldn't be sorry she asked, but maybe if he gave another lightweight sort of answer like the first one, it would alleviate some of the seriousness from their day together. She couldn't shake the feeling that she was tumbling headlong into a relationship with Cal that would leave her with a heartache she'd never forget.

Cal continued. "After you got out of your car—"

"You noticed the first part while I was still in my *car*?" She remembered her first trip to his garage vividly. She'd been in town all of a month when the Honda had started acting up.

Lucky for her, she'd stumbled upon Cal's garage. Not only had she gotten her car fixed, she'd walked away with enough daydream material for the next month.

His grin was unrepentant. "Men make those kind of judgments sort of fast, Maddy."

She sighed.

"Anyway, after you got out of the car I noticed the mountains of textbooks and periodicals in your back seat. Then we talked about how you were starting work on your Master's, and that's when I *really* noticed you."

Madeline still waited for the other shoe to drop. What had he noticed?

He rubbed one hand across her collarbone to cup her shoulder. "There's just something incredibly sexy about how smart you are."

Her heart fluttered in that very unwanted, dreamy way again. How could she not adore a man who wanted her for her brain?

It suddenly struck her that Cal wouldn't care if she kept the boatload of cosmetics the salesperson at the mall had talked her into buying. For that matter, she probably didn't even need the black leather with a guy like Cal.

In fact, the proof that he liked her just the way she was had probably surfaced when he showed up at her doorstep this morning and hadn't even cringed at the sight of her in her oldest pjs.

This man—who'd had his pick of gorgeous women—wanted *her*. Madeline Watson, class nerd.

And if she didn't start running right now, she'd be in love with him before she could say "pocket protector."

13

CAL GAZED into Maddy's eyes and feared he had admitted too much. In an unguarded moment he'd revealed a level of attraction he had managed to keep to himself until now.

He allowed his gaze to slide away from hers, knowing something momentous had just passed between them. He peered around her living room to distract himself, all the while wondering what had just happened.

Yes, he'd just experienced the most deeply satisfying sex of his life. And he was pretty damn sure he'd pleased Maddy, too. But beyond that, he could have sworn the whole world had somehow shifted in the few hours he had been in this room, and he wasn't altogether sure it had anything to do with the off-the-charts sex.

Searching the landscape of her house, he spied a snapshot of her and her father in a polished pewter frame over her bookcase. She was about eight years old, neat and pretty with a starched cotton shirt and a pink ribbon in her hair, glasses perched on her little nose even then.

Cal thought about the way she looked now, with heavy-lidded eyes and mouth swollen from his kiss, her hair wound around them both. He'd distracted her from her smart, good-girl ways. She probably would be putting together her knock-'em-dead proposal for her dissertation right now if he hadn't shown up on her doorstep this morning.

Damn. In his grand scheme to seduce Maddy with as much fervor as she'd seduced him, he'd never stopped to think about what would happen next. What should he do now? Apologize for messing up her hair and spilling a little raspberry juice on the couch?

He'd known all along this couldn't lead to anything permanent. Marriage had taught him he wasn't cut out for long-term emotional investment. He'd only end up disappointing Maddy the same way he'd disappointed his wife.

"Maddy—"

He was saved from having to say anything intelligent by the sound of voices outside her front door.

Voices.

Her eyes flew to his, their gazes crashing together in a look of mutual horror.

"You expecting anyone?" he whispered, reaching for his jeans.

She shook her head, wide-eyed.

Tossing her pajamas toward her, he pulled on his pants. He kicked the excess clothing under the couch as Professor Rose Marie Blakely's voice sounded outside.

"Hey, Maddy, your dissertation is saved!" Dr. Rose called through the door, then spoke in a lower voice to her companion.

The duo on the doorstep laughed, a deep male chuckle followed by a feminine giggle.

Madeline moved in slow motion as she pulled on her pajama bottoms and combed her fingers through her hair. She squinted toward the door.

"It's Rose," Maddy announced, her voice thin and wavering. She sounded as helpless as he felt.

Cal scrambled for her glasses and rested them on her nose. "I know."

"What do I do?" Her words were muffled as she dragged her shirt over her head.

Rose Marie knocked at the door. "Madeline!" Her voice sounded less friendly, and more authoritative this time around. "I've got Dr. Rafferty with me."

Cal had never seen Maddy cry, but she looked damn close to tears now.

This would cause the scandal of the decade: University Professor Debauches Graduate Student. The headline wouldn't care that Maddy taught at Louisville, too. They'd make the most of the fact that she was still pursuing a degree.

"You want me to hide?" He swallowed his pride for her sake. And Allison's. He didn't want to think what his stupidity would cost his sister.

She blanched. "You can't. Your car's here!"

The panic in her voice told him she wouldn't get through this without him. He'd messed up, and he was going to have to pay for it.

"Madeline?" Rose Marie called.

Cal took a deep breath, knowing he had to stay by her side. "Want me to answer the door?"

She shook her head with a quick, jerky movement. "I can get it," she said, her voice whisper-soft. She squeezed his hand before turning toward the door and squaring her shoulders.

"Coming!" she called, moving toward the small foyer.

Cal didn't know what else to do, so he paced the living room floor, every muscle in his body coiled with tension.

Madeline unbolted the latch and cracked the door a few inches.

He strained to hear her words without much success. He had no problem hearing Rose Marie Blakely, however, as Madeline's supervisor edged closer.

"...just go get some clothes on and we'll wait here." The professor's voice floated closer as she maneuvered her way around Maddy. "Whose car is out front?"

Cal paused in his pacing. Maddy stood, immobile, at the front door.

Professor Blakely stepped into the living room. "I mean, I hope we didn't—" Her words faltered along with her footfall. Her gaze locked with Cal's.

Dr. Michael Rafferty stepped in behind her, still oblivious to the awkward situation awaiting him. A long-tenured university fixture, Rafferty had a reputation for being somewhat of a loose cannon. Cal had never met the man personally, even though the sociology professor often taught an evening class in the same building as Cal.

This would make for a hell of an introduction.

The man smiled warmly at Madeline. "Hope we aren't interrupting anything. Rose assured me you make a habit of working on Sundays."

Rose Marie cleared her throat. "Except for today, I guess."

Before Rafferty could look askance at his colleague, he did a double take as his eyes lit upon Cal.

Cal guessed his morning's activities were blatantly obvious. Their breakfast had scattered everywhere. Incriminating pineapple pieces lay on the floor. Madeline's high color, skewed clothing and wild hair pretty much gave her away to any semi-observant bystander.

The fact that she wore no bra probably didn't escape the professor's shrewd eye, either.

Cal cringed as the aging academic flipped open the shades on his small, wire-framed glasses to inspect Madeline at close range.

Cal stepped forward. "If the three of you have business to discuss, I can make myself scarce." He didn't want to desert Maddy in an awkward social situation, but if he could ease the tension for her by leaving, he would.

Rose Marie virtually jumped out of the way of the door to clear a path. "We would only need a few minutes."

Cal sensed an ally in this woman. Could escape be as simple as walking out the door? He braved a glance at Maddy. Her barely perceptible nod told him to go for it.

But before he could think of a suitable exit line, Rafferty leaned closer to him.

"Don't I know you?" he asked.

Myriad curses resounded in Cal's head, impairing his ability to form an intelligible answer.

Allison hadn't even come close to being this busted

when she sneaked out of the house last week. Cal was now officially ensnared in an impossible situation.

Rose Marie interceded in Cal's silence. "You know, Mike, maybe we ought to discuss this tomorrow—"

Rafferty snapped his fingers. "I've got it. You teach the class after mine in Honors Hall."

Cal waited for righteous indignation or maybe an outraged reproach.

Instead Michael Rafferty pointed an accusing finger at Rose Marie. "Ha! Everyone told *me* the teachers couldn't sleep with graduate students. Don't the rules apply to this young man?"

Cal could see Maddy's flush from her collar to her hair roots.

Damn. This was all his fault.

Rose Marie sighed. "Of course the rules apply. The university frowns on this sort of thing." She looked back and forth between Cal and Maddy, regret plainly written in her eyes. "You should probably discuss this with your department chair, Mr. Turner."

Dr. Rafferty cast a grave look in Cal's direction. "The implication being, you need to mention it before we do."

Jaw clenched, Cal grit his teeth. His opinion of the professor sank with each passing minute. "I understood the implication. Thanks."

Rafferty nodded. "I have to admit I find it surprising that I arrived here to discuss a dissertation on mating rituals and stumbled across the primary research process in action."

Maddy didn't flinch, but Cal knew she would feel those words like a blow. He ached for the embarrassment she must be experiencing, and at the same time he damned himself for subjecting her to this. Her reputation had been pristine until he'd rang her bell this morning.

Thankfully, Rose Marie chose that moment to open Maddy's front door and nudge Dr. Rafferty—forcefully—toward the exit. "Come on, Mike, we can discuss this project on Monday."

Rafferty had barely taken two steps when he halted again. "We might not be discussing anything on Monday depending how the administration reacts to this incident." He turned to Madeline, his gaze dipping well below eye level. "Your dissertation won't be an issue if they decide to revoke your assistantship."

Madeline's hand flew to her mouth, perhaps to smother a gasp. Maybe even a scream.

Cal couldn't imagine what she'd do without her position at U of L. Her job meant everything to her.

Maddy turned to Rose Marie. "Could they really do that?" Her voiced wavered. "Could they kick me right out of the program?"

Rose Marie glared at her companion before gently patting Maddy's shoulder. "I don't think they would do something so drastic. You've always had an outstanding reputation in the department."

"But they could," Rafferty pointed out as he finally headed through the door.

Rose Marie mouthed "I'm sorry," to Madeline and Cal, then followed her colleague.

Rafferty's voice drifted back to them as Rose Marie joined him on the way to the car. "Sign me up for her review committee if they don't give her the boot, Rose.

I'll bet she writes the hottest dissertation this university has ever seen.''

Cal's fingers flexed into a fist as Rafferty's sly chuckle faded in the distance.

Madeline slammed the door behind them, clearly overhearing every word as well as Cal had. He reached for her waist to hold her, then stopped himself.

She might not welcome his touch after what had just happened. He wouldn't fault her if she blamed him for the whole debacle. He was the one who had tracked her down and bribed his way inside with breakfast. He was the one who hadn't been able to keep his hands off her.

And now Maddy would pay the price. Her dissertation project probably didn't stand a chance. Her upstanding reputation had been compromised to such an extent that she might lose her position.

They hadn't been just caught kissing on campus. No, they'd been discovered half-dressed in Maddy's house—a flagrant scenario Madeline had probably never dreamed of when she'd first envisioned ways to tilt her good-girl halo a little.

But all along, Cal had recognized the fiery potential of her naive scheme. And instead of talking her out of it, he'd taken her seductive techniques to new heights—and the consequences to new depths.

Despite his recent degree and his glorified teaching job, he'd still managed to screw up the big things in life. Beneath it all, he was still a mechanic from backwoods Tennessee.

Even worse, he'd betrayed his sister's trust by jeopardizing her future. What judge would grant guardianship to a teacher who seduced a graduate student? No matter that Maddy was a consenting adult, had never been his student, or that they'd known each other long before Cal started teaching.

The whole thing sounded sordid enough to give credence to Delia Heywood's claims and to force the social services department to stamp "Rejected" all over his custody request.

He looked around Maddy's living room, the evidence of their decadent morning reminding him that he'd brought all of this down on their heads. Her pale face and wide eyes completed the image of the upheaval he'd wrought. He had to get out of here before he made things worse. Before he did something stupid such as take her in his arms and offer her more than comfort.

"I'd better go," he muttered, searching the dining room table for his keys.

Madeline spied the keys and snatched them up before he had the chance. She squeezed the cool metal in her hands, allowing the rough edges to dig into her flesh.

No way would she let him walk out on her after the nightmare they'd just been through.

"Not yet." She didn't think she could face the rest of this day until they sat and talked about the jumbled mess of their relationship.

She gestured to the tray of fruit by her couch and attempted to make light of a bad situation. "We haven't made a dent in the food."

Cal scrubbed his hand over his jaw, as if contemplating how to obtain his keys. "Don't you think we've done enough damage for one day?"

"I'm sorry about all of this. I know it will hurt Allison's guardianship hearing, and I can't tell you how awful I feel." She should have known better than to let him stay for a brunch she had zero chance of resisting. But now that the worst had happened, what did it matter if they at least talked about where to go next?

"This could nullify the guardianship hearing, Maddy." He spent restless energy folding up the paper bags littering her table. "I need to come up with a strategy for how I'm going to handle this."

"Isn't that something we should do together?" She tried appealing to him as his friend.

He stacked the bags and weighted the pile with a bowl of fake fruit she used as a centerpiece. "I think we're going to need to approach this separately, Maddy. We've both got a lot at stake here."

Forget approaching him as his friend. She swayed closer and wound her fingers around his shoulders, hoping her touch would mean more to him than logic. "All the more reason for us to work on this together! Maybe if we—"

He stepped back, out of her embrace. "There is no 'we,' Maddy." He walked to the other side of the table, as if he couldn't insert enough space between them. "I screwed up and I'm sorry. But I've got to get home and talk to Allison before she catches wind of this from someone else."

Madeline stared at him, knowing the hurt ripping through her was only a precursor to what she'd feel once he left for good.

Cal held out his palm. "So if you'll just give me my keys..."

She'd almost forgotten she held them. Careful not to touch him again, she relinquished them into his hand. She noticed the shape of the keys remained outlined on her flesh, a small dent compared to the impression he'd left on the rest of her.

Having retrieved his ticket to freedom, Cal headed for the door. He paused on her Welcome mat. "I never meant for this to happen."

"You had no way of knowing," Madeline assured him, wishing she could make him feel just a little bit better. "Rose Marie has never come over on a weekend before. Besides, you weren't the one looking for trouble, Cal. I shouldn't have dragged you into my quest for...experience."

Cal jingled the keys in his palm, but didn't open the door. "It's been a little more than a quest, don't you think?"

She smiled to keep herself from crying. "If it had been more than that, I don't think you'd be leaving right now."

He stared down at the woven doormat for a long moment and then pulled open the door. "Sorry, Maddy. You'll navigate your way through this better without me here. And I've got to talk to Allison."

She'd never needed someone so much as she needed him right now. It teetered on her tongue to tell him as much.

But she couldn't.

Her reserved, scholarly side, the one that had protected her from messy emotional entanglements ever since childhood, refused to let her confide her feelings to Cal.

The beat of his boots on her front step echoed through her as surely as he'd trounced his way across her heart. She stood over her dining room table, listening to the sounds of his car starting, followed by the low rumble of the engine fading into the distance.

She took a seat at the table, her whole body so brittle she feared it might break if she moved too fast. She ran an idle finger over the paper bags Cal had folded so meticulously, and struggled to process everything that had happened to her since this morning.

The best day of her life had turned into the worst, and Madeline wasn't sure how long she had before the numbness would wear off and she'd be left with just the hurt.

She could have endured the professional consequences of her liaison with Cal. Although her father would have been devastated, Madeline was learning that a career could not be the sum total of her existence. She needed more in her life than her studies, and she didn't want to wait to obtain it until she had ten different degrees on the wall. She wanted to find that extra something—or someone—now.

The threat to her academic standing she could deal with. But she wasn't at all sure if she could cope with Cal leaving.

Watching him walk out the door had assured her she was her father's daughter. Her father hadn't been able to juggle a career and a personal life, and it now seemed pretty obvious she couldn't, either.

Heck, she couldn't handle either one. She'd just ruined both of hers in one swoop.

Her gaze strayed to the fruit on the ottoman in the living room. The pile of raspberries had been diminished more than any of the others.

An image of her and Cal tangled on the couch flashed through her mind.

Things had been going so well this morning. Where might their relationship have led if not for their untimely interruption?

Would they have decided to rendezvous again? Perhaps they would have devised another secret tryst so their relationship could remain uncomplicated and discreet.

Some discretion.

Maybe they should have just gone out on a regular date like the rest of the single population and faced the consequences at the university openly. Cal had tried to tell her they should go on a real date. But Madeline had been so caught up in her career goals that she'd wanted either a tawdry romance to flaunt around campus, or a low-maintenance friendship that wouldn't interfere with her work.

All the while, she'd ignored the possibilities of the middle ground. They could have found a way to see each other legitimately. Maybe if they'd discussed their situation with the administration ahead of time, they could have found a simple resolution or a reprieve on the edict against student-teacher relationships.

She and Cal could have gotten to know each other all over again, this time as more than just friends.

Apparently, she had more in common with her father than she'd first realized. Her own academic snobbery had made her choose work over Cal.

And she only recognized her mistake after it was too late to fix. Cal couldn't put enough distance between them now that she'd probably ruined his chance of gaining guardianship for Allison.

Overall, she couldn't have picked a more rotten time to realize she was in love with Cal.

14

MADELINE HAD NEVER BEEN so grateful for a Monday morning. After a fitful night with no sleep and plenty of panic attacks, she'd come up with only one possible solution to her current dilemma.

As soon as nine o'clock rolled around, she would march into Rose Marie's office and resign her teaching assistantship.

Amazingly, the world hadn't crashed to an end when she'd arrived at that decision. Once she'd admitted to herself she cared more about Cal than achieving the most stellar career any sociologist had ever seen, her choice had been obvious.

Cal needed to stay in town because of his business. But Maddy could move.

She'd relocated to Louisville on a lark, just because it sounded pretty. Even though she'd grown to love her adopted home, she could find another university comparable to U of L. The University of Kentucky was only an hour away. She could always transfer there if she wanted—or if someone else wanted her—to stay in the state.

Although Cal might be just as glad to see her and her high heels head as far out of town as possible.

A boundless ache stabbed through her at the thought of never seeing Cal again.

Madeline drove into work, snapping her gum without much enthusiasm, battling a somber mood. She didn't mind sacrificing a few months of her studies so that Allison's guardianship would be approved without a hitch. Madeline could be in a new program by the spring semester if she started applying right away.

The thought of leaving Cal continued to weigh on her, however. Deep inside, she still nurtured a tiny hope that he wouldn't want her to go. Maybe he'd just been upset yesterday when he'd walked out, and today he would feel differently.

She remembered his failed marriage then, and the fact that Cal had told her more than once he'd never marry again. What kind of future could there have been for them anyway if Cal wasn't willing to trust his heart to another woman?

Still, it would hurt unbearably if he let her go without a blink.

Checking the clock tower as she pulled in the parking lot, Madeline arrived right on schedule. She had just enough time to swing by Human Resources to deliver a copy of her resignation letter before she met with Rose Marie to announce her news.

Madeline stared down at her penny loafers as she crossed campus, hoping she wouldn't hear any snippets of gossip about her and Cal along the way. She had no doubt yesterday's incident would be the object of much discussion.

She pulled open the door to a side entrance of the administration building, hoping there weren't too many people lined up at the main desk. She turned the corner leading to the lobby and found Cal Turner already at the counter, speaking to a pretty administrative assistant.

The young woman behind the desk nodded at whatever he was saying. "No problem, Mr. Turner," she said as she batted long eyelashes at him. "I'll file your resignation through all the necessary channels. We'll just drop your last check in the mail."

Madeline froze.

He couldn't quit. He, unlike Madeline, didn't have the option of packing his trunk and leaving town. He needed to stay here.

"Cal, wait." Finding her voice, she scrambled over to the counter. "Don't do this."

CAL WAVED AWAY THE WOMAN he'd been speaking to just as Maddy's hand clutched his arm. He closed his eyes to brace himself for a confrontation he hadn't prepared for. Her touch reminded him that they'd spent half of yesterday tangled on her living room couch, but he damn well couldn't afford to travel that path again.

Too much potential for heartache.

He took a deep breath and turned to face her. "Hi, Maddy."

She looked sleep-deprived and worried. Her cheeks lacked the definite pink hue he'd placed there yesterday. Her eyebrows knit together, and even her glasses couldn't hide the dark circles under her eyes.

"What are you doing?" Her hushed voice reached a higher octave, fraught with concern.

He pulled her around the corner, away from the main desk. "I'm quitting, Maddy. It's the only thing I *can* do."

She straightened her shirt from where he'd tugged on her arm. "No it's not, because *I'm* quitting." She pulled a white envelope out of her book bag and gestured with it as she spoke. "You can ask the desk to give you your letter back, Cal, because I'm giving my notice right now."

"No, Maddy." Where had she come up with such a crazy idea?

"Yes, Cal."

He sighed. He sure hadn't anticipated this.

Still, his heart warmed at her gesture. No one had ever given up anything for him before. His parents, much as he loved them, had never put their children before their own interests. His mother's love of money still meant more to her than the people in her life. And his dad had always been too busy with his motorcycles and chasing women to pay much attention to Cal.

Even his wife hadn't been willing to compromise her lifestyle once they'd married. She'd walked out on him once her lust for him had been appeased, saying she needed to maintain a more upscale lifestyle than Cal could afford at the time.

But respectable, honorable Madeline Watson cared enough about him to sacrifice her position for him.

"No," he repeated, sliding the envelope out of her hands, then tucking it back into her bag.

She glared at him. "What do you mean, no? It's a fact, Cal. I'm resigning so we don't both end up with tainted professional records. You need to stay here because of Allison and your business, but I can go someplace else to work on my degree."

"Not in this lifetime, you won't." How could she

think he would let her do this? He tugged her a little further down the hall and out the side entrance so they could speak privately. "Maddy, you love Louisville. You have a house here. You've already won the respect of your colleagues and your students. You can't just walk away from that."

"And you can?" The coil of her hair slipped further back on her head as she spoke.

He hadn't seen her so fired up since the university turned down her dissertation—and even then, she'd been more upset than full of passionate conviction.

She poked an accusatory finger at his chest. "I thought this job meant more to you than a paycheck. I thought you started teaching because you couldn't wait to share the secrets to success with other people."

"I did." No doubt he would miss the classroom. Teaching gave him a sense of self-worth that all his business accomplishments had never managed.

But Maddy's happiness came first.

Cal fought the urge to touch her, willing her to understand. Her honey-brown eyes seemed to close out the rest of the world, narrowing his focus to nothing but her.

He gave her the bottom line. "I'm going to take a couple of years hiatus to give you time to finish up your degree."

And to give himself plenty of distance. Yesterday's brunch had proven he had zero resolve where the Lady Scholar was concerned. He refused to mess up her career any more than he already had.

He might lose Maddy for good, but at least he would have made this right for her.

"But—"

"I've got to go, Maddy." He needed to start putting space between them—pronto. Two more hours and he'd head down to Tennessee to try to iron a few things out concerning Allison's guardianship. Now that he'd quit the job at U of L, he needed to talk to the social services people in his sister's native state to see how things stood for the hearing. Maybe he could even soften Delia's heart if he showed up in her driveway without the Harley.

He rushed his words so she couldn't interrupt. He needed to make this break as fast as possible before he changed his mind. "I'm already late for an appointment at the garage this morning. Don't worry about this anymore." He backed away, ignoring the pang in his gut at the thought of never touching her again. "Everything's taken care of."

Madeline couldn't believe he would walk away from her twice in two days, especially after all they'd shared together. But sure enough, Cal seemed content to take care of everything on his own and expect her to accept it.

He even tossed her a wave as he left.

"We'll see about that," she muttered, unwilling to let him steamroll over her with the force of his charismatic personality.

She could still give her notice today and talk to Cal about it after the fact. He'd go back to his job if she left town.

Too bad she'd leave her heart behind with her high-handed best friend.

Battling tears, Madeline made her way to Fultz Hall

to find Rose Marie, blind to the comfort the dignified buildings of her academic world usually imparted. Madeline didn't think she could get through the day without unburdening herself to someone. Cal didn't have the time or the inclination to hear her out this morning, it seemed.

The scent of peppermint beckoned from Rose Marie's door as Madeline knocked.

"Come in," her friend called.

Pushing the frosted-glass door open, Madeline edged her way inside Rose Marie's cramped office. Books lined every wall while overflow stacks littered the floor. Photographs from around the world decorated the shelves and camouflaged the back of the computer terminal.

"Can we talk?" Madeline tossed her book bag on a nearby chair, dismayed to hear the quaver in her voice.

Rose Marie frowned. "Of course, Maddy. I tried to call you last night but your phone just rang and rang. I'm so, so sorry about walking in on you yesterday."

Madeline shrugged. She'd been too busy crying and eating her way through a quart of fudge ripple ice cream to pick up any call that didn't have Cal's name on the caller ID. "It's okay."

"No, it isn't. I shouldn't have just dropped by like that."

Madeline waved away her friend's concern, more upset about today's events than yesterday's. "We talk all the time on Sunday mornings and I've never had a guy at my house once in the four years you've known me." Madeline's track record had been so squeaky-clean, no one expected her to have a life outside school.

"I'm sure it never occurred to you I might have some-one there."

Rose Marie flipped her long blond hair behind one shoulder and sighed. "Still, it was wrong of me, and I'm sorry."

Madeline slumped into the chair across from her. "So I take it you had convinced Dr. Rafferty to join the dissertation committee and maybe swing the vote in my favor?"

"I thought we could make a good case for replacing one of the other professors who doesn't have as much interest in your topic." Rose Marie blew across the surface of her steaming tea. "Mike Rafferty taught human sexuality for two years at another university, so I thought he'd be a good addition to the committee."

Madeline nodded. "He did seem rather...open-minded about the whole sex thing."

Rose Marie rolled her eyes. "He instigated a big 'the-oretical' discussion one night in the lounge about the gray area of sleeping with a graduate student, and everyone in the room jumped down his throat."

"I think it's a little different with me and Cal—"

"It's nothing like you and Cal. Cal's not full-time fac-ulty, he's not in your program, he's never been your teacher." She counted the list off on her fingers. "And you two had a friendship in place before he even started here."

Madeline relaxed a little, relieved she wasn't the only one who didn't see anything disreputable about her relationship with Cal.

"Rafferty is just a bit of an instigator. I don't think he liked the idea that someone else on campus could get away with something off limits for him." She sipped her tea and peered over the desk at Madeline.

Madeline sniffled. "It doesn't matter now anyway because Cal just quit."

"How thoughtful!" Rose Marie smiled her approval.

"No, how awful," Madeline mumbled.

"He's a businessman first and foremost, Madeline. Teaching has always just been a sideline for him."

"I can't let him leave because of me." Madeline fished in her bag for her resignation. Seizing it, she flung the missive across Rose Marie's desk. "I'm quitting, not him."

Her program chair made no move to touch the paper. "I can't accept this, Maddy."

Madeline shoved the document closer to Rose Marie. "You most certainly can. Cal needs this job."

"He needs it?" Rose Marie quirked a perfectly arched blond brow. "The man doesn't just operate a storefront, Madeline, he owns a *chain* of prosperous businesses. I think he'll manage to pay the rent without his two classes a week here."

"You don't understand!" Madeline slapped the desktop with her hand, causing the tea to ripple in its cup. "Cal has it in his head that being a mechanic isn't good enough. This job gives him a validation that he doesn't find in his day-to-day work."

Slowly, Rose Marie nodded. "Maybe he only thought he needed the validation to impress you."

Why would he ever think something like that?

"No," Madeline replied. "Cal genuinely enjoys teaching."

"It was just a thought." Rose Marie shrugged and

passed Madeline's letter back to her. "But I'm not accepting your resignation when you've got a lecture hall filled with fifty freshmen to teach this morning, Maddy. There's no way I'm setting foot in a Sociology 101 classroom to cover for you."

Madeline took the letter and tucked it inside her book bag, frustration nagging at her from every direction. "Okay, but you haven't heard the end of this. I'm going to talk to Cal later, and make him see reason." Why did he have to thwart her one effort to do something nice for him? She'd been putting her career before everything else in her life for long enough.

She wasn't about to let him cut ties to a teaching position he loved. His students deserved to hear his lectures, especially when he taught such practical things as how to make a living.

Madeline's academic aspirations centered around the mating process—something everyone but her seemed to be familiar with anyway. Her work, while definitely interesting, lacked the real-life importance of Cal's.

Rose Marie twirled her fountain pen and eyed Madeline. "This may not be any of my business, Maddy, but I'm going to go ahead and ask anyway. How did you snag the most sought-after man on campus? Because if it had anything to do with the red dress and the awesome makeup job I did the other night, I want some credit."

Sensual memories washed over Madeline, taunting her with the knowledge that Cal wanted nothing better than to put distance between them.

"The red dress definitely helped." Although maybe

not in the way Rose Marie imagined. Madeline credited her outfit with giving her the courage to explore an adventurous side she'd never known she possessed.

"I knew it!"

Madeline couldn't help but smile. "Cal told me he liked me even before the red dress though."

Rose Marie sighed dreamily. "You have to admire a man who sees beyond the surface."

Madeline did more than admire him. She wavered somewhere between "head over sensible heels" and the point of no return.

"You're crazy about him, aren't you?"

"Certifiable." She sniffed back her tears, searching her bag for a tissue.

Rose Marie murmured sympathetically, then reached in her desk and withdrew a pack of gum and a packet of Kleenex tissues. "Here, honey."

"Thanks."

"Was it your first time?"

Madeline stiffened. Some women shared their every sordid secret, but she had never been one of them.

Rose Marie laughed and reached over the desk to pat Madeline's hand. "I mean, is this the first time you've been in love?"

"Oh. Yes." Maybe Rose Marie could offer helpful advice on how to make the gnawing ache in her chest disappear. "Is it always this awful?"

"For me it has been." Rose Marie flipped her long hair over one shoulder. "None of the men I've dated understand my commitment to work."

Madeline knew a man who would understand perfectly. She wondered if Rose Marie would consider dating a physics genius whose heart had always been in the right place. Dr. Watson would definitely be impressed by Rose's ivy league credentials, and Rose Marie could help Madeline loosen her dad up a bit.

She made a mental note to invite her father back to Louisville soon.

"But I've been more unlucky than most," Rose Marie continued, oblivious to Madeline's cupid machinations. "And Cal Turner strikes me as a good guy, despite his reputation."

"He dated a lot after his divorce, but I think those were extenuating circumstances." She knew he'd been torn up about his wife's defection when she'd first met him. And his dating schedule seemed to settle down a lot a year or so later.

"Definitely forgivable. I think you'd be crazy to *not* fall for him. If a guy like Cal looked at me, I'd be trying to figure out how to get closer to him, not trying to quit my job and run away from him."

"That's not what I'm doing."

"No?" Rose Marie rotated her teacup, then peered inside. "My tea leaves tell me different."

"I'm not running," Madeline repeated, realizing how much she meant it. "I want to be with Cal."

"Have you told him as much?"

Ouch. Talk about baring your soul. "That sounds painful."

"Only if he doesn't reciprocate."

Which he didn't. He wouldn't have walked out yesterday if he'd felt the same way about her. "I think I'll spare myself the heartache. I already know how he feels."

Rose Marie flashed her a reassuring smile. "Love is all about risk, Maddy. If you try to spare yourself the heartache, you haven't really taken the plunge."

Madeline couldn't help but think Cal would never stand still long enough for her to take the plunge. He'd become an expert at making himself scarce.

She departed Rose Marie's office far more confused than she'd entered. Half an hour ago she'd had a purpose—quit her job so Cal could stay at his. Now she didn't know what to do.

Cal had walked out on her last night, then quit his job without warning today. He might not want to see her, but now that he'd gone and made her fall in love with him, he didn't really have a choice. She would have things out with him, and she would find a way to make him stay at U of L.

The idea of exposing her heart to him flitted through her mind, daring her to take her biggest risk yet. She'd already managed the singles scene and stilettos. She'd stood up to her father for the first time in her life, and next she was even going to take a stand with her dissertation committee.

Even at her most daring, mini-skirted best, however, Madeline Watson had never bared her heart and soul to anyone. But maybe, with Cal Turner as incentive, she'd find a way to face her biggest challenge yet.

CAL STOOD OVER his answering machine, patting Duchess's head and listening to the week's worth of messages that had piled up at his house in his absence.

The Lady Scholar had apparently been hunting for him all week and by the time her third message played,

Cal could tell by her voice she was mad. Although he'd taken his cell phone and forwarded his business calls, he'd never thought to check his home messages while he was in Tennessee. The only people who ever called the house were Allison's friends.

He dialed Maddy's office and left a message, all the while telling himself to not be too optimistic about her calls. Although part of him had hoped she'd be just a little touched by him resigning, he knew she had probably returned to business as usual at her office.

She might have just called for some closure on their time together. Or maybe she just wanted to say goodbye.

Perhaps that was the real reason he hadn't checked the messages at his house. He hadn't wanted to finalize his farewells with Maddy yet. No matter how much he told himself he had no business being with a highbrow intellectual destined for a doctorate, he'd thought about her all week.

And somewhere between Knoxville and the Kentucky state line, he'd realized he loved her.

The notion still blew him away.

He'd tried to remind himself of his divorce, and what a nightmare that had been. He hadn't wanted to fall in love anytime soon, and he definitely hadn't wanted to think in terms of marriage ever again, but two weeks with Maddy Watson generated thoughts of both.

He tossed on work clothes and headed for the garage, too keyed up to do anything but wrestle with a motor. He had an early model Corvette engine he'd been restoring in his spare time. It was just the sort of greasy, physical labor he needed to cast off thoughts of a certain respectable woman who would have been better off in her ivory tower without him.

Even if she had called him three times.

Damning his runaway thoughts all the way to the converted barn, Cal pulled open the doors and let the sunlight stream over his work space.

He wheeled his tools next to the propped engine, reminding himself why he absolutely would not drive over to Maddy's house uninvited again. She wouldn't be there anyway, for starters. She had office hours until five o'clock on Fridays, and it was only four-thirty.

But most of all, he wouldn't go because no matter how he added up the pluses and minuses of their relationship, he still came away thinking she'd be better off without him. Despite her brief walk on the wild side, Madeline would always be a refined, cultured woman. Cal, on the other hand, would always spend his weekends in his garage, up to his elbows in grease and enjoying every minute of it.

He slid a chair over to the engine to work on it, thinking sooner or later Madeline would begin to feel as if she were missing out on something by staying with him. And sooner or later, she'd walk away just as his first wife had.

Not that he was thinking about her.

He sprayed a few rusty screws to loosen them up and then searched for the right wrenches.

He unscrewed and rescrewed, cleaned and oiled for almost an hour. Several stubborn bolts gave him trouble, but none so much as the thoughts of Maddy. He was about to head inside to call her office again—only because he felt obligated to return her calls and not because he longed to hear the sound of her voice—when the crunch of gravel alerted him to a car turning into his driveway.

It couldn't be Allison, because she'd already left to study at a friend's house.

Curious, Cal set down his wrench and peered outside in time to see a virago in sensible shoes and an oversize buttoned-down shirt leap from a gold Honda and stomp up the drive.

The visitor's hair had come undone from its topknot and slithered around her shoulders to bounce in time with her determined steps. The pinched set of her mouth and the furrow over her brow proclaimed to him she was madder than a wet cat, but he'd never been so glad to see anyone in his life.

He stepped just outside the barn door to meet her.

"Hey, gorgeous," he drawled in his best, fresh-from-Tennessee accent. He might have thought about her every waking—and God knew every non-waking—moment since last Sunday, but if she was here to give their fling a failing mark and move on, he didn't want to seem too eager.

She stopped two feet in front of him and planted her small fists on her hips. The afternoon sun glinted off her brown hair, giving her a golden glow.

"Don't you dare, 'Hey, gorgeous' me, Cal Turner." Her gaze pelted him with evil-eye darts straight through the barrier of her glasses. "You've got exactly one hour to drag yourself over to U of L to teach your Friday night class, or I'm afraid I'm going to have to haul you back to campus myself."

15

A LITTLE OF MADELINE'S steam evaporated when she feasted her eyes on the vision from her past. Cal looked as delicious as the first time she'd seen him, his blue work shirt stretched over muscles that had clearly spent more days jacking up cars than pushing pencils.

His sleeves were rolled up to his elbows, attesting to his labors. He wiped his hands on a towel as she approached, leaving dark prints on the worn white terry cloth.

Madeline wondered what it would be like to be touched by a man who left handprints. The image struck her as very primal, more than a little territorial, and definitely a turn-on.

If she wasn't careful, her anger would turn to lust and then she'd never get anything accomplished today.

And heaven knew, she wasn't leaving here until she got a few things straight with a certain sexy mechanic.

"So what'll it be, Cal? Are you going to head back to the classroom willingly? Or am I going to have to tow you over to campus myself?"

"Sorry. Can't do it. Besides, they've already hired my replacement." He crossed his arms and grinned down at her. "My money says you don't stand a chance of budging me anyway."

"I could if I was mad enough." She'd been pretty angry before she'd found him today, but her ire had faded the moment she'd seen him again. A week apart had been too much. "Care to tell me why you didn't bother returning my calls all week?"

"I went to Tennessee."

"You did?" She'd imagined Cal sitting at home this week, listening to her messages on his machine and not bothering to pick up the phone. It hadn't occurred to her he might have left town. "Why?"

He shrugged. "I needed to file a few papers for Allison's guardianship. I had a long talk with Allison's aunt Delia, too, while I was at it."

"Did it do any good at this late date?" Madeline was surprised. "She couldn't withdraw her motion now, anyway, could she?"

"I don't think so. But that wasn't my point. I just hated to think that she genuinely feared for Allison's well-being while in my care." He flashed her a dimpled grin. "I took my own advice, in fact, and worked up a proposal for her on what life would be like in the Turner household for Allison."

"You're kidding."

Cal shook his head. "And she loved it. She even had me look at her car while I was there, so I think I won her over."

The man could probably charm good grades out of his students. Madeline wished she'd thought to sic him on Aunt Delia before. "But that doesn't help your custody case on Tuesday, does it?"

"Probably not. But I shared my proposal and some other information with social services and it went well.

Looks like the hearing should go off without a hitch and Allison will finally have some closure on a rough chapter in her life."

No doubt Cal had gone to Tennessee to assure social services he'd quit his job to alleviate any fears they might have about his integrity.

Madeline could have told them men didn't get any more honorable than Cal Turner. "What about you?"

"What about me?" He rocked back on his heels, watching her with wary eyes.

She gathered courage and asked him what was on her mind anyway. "Are you still looking for closure on a rough chapter?"

He studied her for so long she almost retracted the question.

"Not necessarily." He scuffed his boot through the loose gravel outside the barn. "I mean, I used the time to think about things, but I wouldn't say I was trying to close any chapters."

Whew. Surely that counted for something. He hadn't come straight out and said he wanted to move beyond their relationship.

He gazed at her steadily. The warm light of the setting sun locked on the shades of green in his eyes, making Madeline see him in a different way than she had before.

"How about you?" he asked.

She shook her head so hard her glasses thumped against her nose. "No closure needed here." She realized they'd never get anywhere if she didn't start laying some emotional cards on the table. If she didn't want him to slip by her, she needed to at least be honest with him.

"But I did try to resolve some of what went on here last weekend. I tried especially hard to quit my job, but Rose Marie wouldn't let me."

"You what?" He stepped closer, threatening to sap all the starch from her spine.

"I tried to resign the assistantship, Cal." She had wanted to do something unselfish for once—to think about him instead of her career. But he'd been a step ahead of her, robbing her of a chance to be gracious. "I can transfer most anywhere that has a Ph.D. program, but your life is here. You deserve to stay."

He frowned. "We went over this on Monday, Maddy. The university is your territory. Always has been." He rested his hands on his hips, broadening the expanse of his body and shielding everything but him from her view.

She couldn't stand this close to him without touching. His chest rested less than a foot away, near enough to trail her fingers over.

"I couldn't..." Her thoughts drifted. She really wanted to. "I mean...I can't stay at U of L, knowing you'd left because of me."

"I'll go back and teach in a couple of years. But until Allison is eighteen I'm going to keep a lower profile. She really needs more time with me, anyway. I was getting a little sapped between my teaching and the stress of Perfect Timing."

"Oh." So much for Madeline's effort to be unselfish. "You'd really transfer somewhere else...for me?"

She rushed on. "I think I could be in a different program as soon as the spring semester. You could still keep your classes. It would be just like you'd been absent."

"I thought you liked it here." He looked almost offended.

"I do, but—"

"And for a northern girl, you're developing a sweet little Kentucky twang."

"You're kidding."

"Yeah." He grinned. "But I keep hoping."

Madeline smiled, and then realized for the first time how Cal's laid-back charm had always made it easy for her to keep their relationship light and undemanding. He could tease her into a better mood or coax a smile from her even on her busiest days. But she wouldn't be satisfied with that anymore.

She'd come here to lay her heart on the line.

Seeing her chance to take a risk, Madeline didn't want Cal to let her off the hook this time. Closing her eyes for a long moment, Madeline jumped in with both feet.

"What I mean to say is that you're more important to me than my job, Cal."

Silence greeted her declaration for a drawn-out moment.

"Look at me, Maddy."

Slowly she raised her eyelids.

He squinted in the sunlight, as if to see her better. "You mean that?"

"I mean it." Having come this far, Maddy took one step further by reaching out to lay a palm on Cal's chest.

She felt him suck in a breath as she did.

"But I thought your career came first until you got the doctorate." He lifted a hand as if to touch her cheek, but his fingers hovered in midair and then fell to his side. "I've known that for as long as I've known you."

"Priorities change." Hers shifted in an instant, although maybe she'd been growing away from her old values for years and just hadn't realized it until now. "I knew last Sunday after you walked out of my house that you mattered to me more than my work. The chances of my dissertation being approved had just been severely compromised, but that seemed like nothing compared to the hurt I felt when you left."

The steady beat of his heart under her palm reassured her.

He shook his head. "Honey, you don't know what you're saying."

"Yes, I do." This was it. Make or break time. "I love you, Cal."

Again, he lifted his hands as if to touch her, then slammed them back down on his hips in frustration.

"Damnation, woman. How can you love a man who can't even touch you because he's covered with grease?" His easy manner vanished as he glared at her. "I've always got grease on my hands, Maddy. I live out here in the boondocks with my dog and my cars and I'll never be right for some uptown professor whose name will be followed by more letters than there are in the alphabet." He stepped back from her, dodging her touch.

She stared at him, trying to recover her balance from

his outburst. When she'd imagined this conversation earlier this week, she had envisioned a more gentle scenario in which he explained to her that he didn't love her in return.

She never guessed her declaration would have him up in arms.

He paced away from her, then suddenly turned back. "And another thing, your father would kill me."

"I think you could handle Daddy, Cal."

He rolled his eyes. "He's your father, Maddy, I'd have to let him kill me. It's a respect thing."

Hope funneled through her. "So you're considering it?"

"What?"

She'd just laid her heart on the line for him. How could he be so obtuse? "Liking me in return?"

He crossed the driveway to stand nose-to-nose with her. "Honey, I want you so bad it's been killing me all week. I want to unbutton that crazy shirt with my teeth and make love to you until we're both delirious, then lay down by your side until you come to your senses."

She swallowed. All her nerve endings leaped to alert, wishing Cal would make good on his words.

"But that's the bad news, Maddy," he continued. "You *will* come to your senses one day, and you'll decide you no longer see the appeal of a simple guy who spends half his day up to his elbows in grease."

"Is that what you think?" Her heart pounded with new fury, her lust sliding away in a rare fit of anger.

"That's what I think."

"Then let me tell you something, Cal. In case you haven't noticed, I am not some untouchable princess who walks around in silk and satin every day. I'm pretty much a cotton kind of girl."

Maddy thought he might have winced at that statement, but she was too mad to be sure.

"I don't know where you got the idea that I'm some sort of uptight goody-goody, but you're dead wrong. Because looking at those hands of yours right now, all I can see are the talented instruments of your trade, and the fingers that teased me to the best orgasm of my life, and the palms I want planted all over me right now." She plucked up one hand and jammed it squarely against her waist.

Cal stared back at her, eyes wide.

His hand would no doubt stain her white buttondown. But she didn't care one bit. She wanted nothing more than for him to take possession of her in every way imaginable right now, and if he left handprints in the process, so much the better.

She lifted his other hand.

"Honey, you don't have to—"

And positioned it just over her left breast.

"Oh, Maddy."

She closed her eyes, her senses attuning to Cal's touch as his palms soothed her frustration and thrilled her senses. Her anger dissipated faster than it had arrived, leaving behind an acute hunger for Cal and a lingering fear that he wouldn't return her love.

Her eyes flew open as Cal started to pull his hands away from her body. She searched his features for a hint of his feelings, but he only stared down at her white shirt and the two handprints he'd left behind.

And then he smiled.

"I can't believe you." He settled his hands at her waist and stepped closer. "You've got a wild streak a mile wide, woman, and I don't think it has anything to do with the leather miniskirt."

Her heart rate kicked up a hopeful notch. "See? I'm not just a doctorate and a dissertation, Cal. I want more in my life than that."

He nodded, absorbing her words. "Like Sunday brunches?"

"Definitely."

"And an occasional night on the town?"

"Next time I'll be glued to your side."

His palms clenched her hips and pulled her to him. "Honey, I love the way you think almost as much as I love you."

Her heart paused and her whole body quieted to be sure she'd heard him correctly.

"You love me?" She wanted it to be true. She couldn't imagine the kinds of rewards Cal's love would bring. She'd never met a more generous-hearted man.

"I love you, Madeline." His gaze connected with hers, assuring her how much he meant it. "And I love your bulky clothes and your glasses and all those fancy, smart words you use."

He bent his head to hers for a long, hungry kiss. "And the way you taste," he murmured, trailing his lips down the column of her throat.

Her skin tingled and tightened, eager for more than he could give her in his driveway.

"I want you, Maddy." His body pressed up against hers, revealing exactly how much he wanted her. "I want nothing more than to head upstairs for a trial wedding night—"

"Wedding night?" A little spectrum of fanciful visions from girlhood arose in her mind. Orange blossoms and lilies, a long, lacy veil, and falling into the arms of a man who would love her no matter what.

She pulled back to see if he was kidding.

"You heard me, gorgeous. I hope you're in the mood for a white dress because I don't intend to compromise your respectable reputation any longer than I have to." His hands kneaded the notch of her waist. "But Allison and I come as a package deal, you know. Two Turners for the price of one."

She practically toppled him over when she jumped into his arms. "Yes!" Marriage to her closest friend and only lover sounded absolutely right. She'd belong to a family of people who hugged and kissed each other for no reason, a family who supported each other. Maybe with their combined efforts, they'd inspire her father to open his arms a little wider, too.

Madeline squeezed Cal's shoulders, overwhelmed with the payoff of her risk today. By baring her soul to Cal, she'd won the love of a man who'd never let her go.

She giggled. "And I'll get a sister in the deal! I've always wanted a sister."

He pressed his lips to her forehead with gentle reverence. "That's settled then. We're heading down the aisle before Christmas and I'll just learn to survive two geniuses in the same household, I guess."

An idea pounced upon her. She framed his face with

her hands. "If we are married, we can both teach. You don't have to quit!"

He cuffed her wrists in his hands and locked them in place. "No. I'm taking the next two years off to spend time with my family."

She wanted to tell him that he didn't need to make sacrifices for her sake, but he silenced her with a kiss.

Only when she was too dazed to speak did he come up for air.

"Maddy, I meant what I said about concentrating on the home front until Allison's eighteen. And now that I'll have a new bride to please..." He pulled her arms around his neck and grinned. "I'll be way too exhausted to hold down two jobs."

He kissed her, long, slow, and meltingly, until Madeline recalled their whereabouts and pulled back a step.

"Let me just go call Allison to tell her we are going for a drive," Cal suggested, refusing to let go of her hips. "Better yet, I'll call her from the cell phone. Maybe we could go back to your place."

She frowned. "I don't know, Cal, you're really a mess."

He tugged her toward him again. "I'll wash up before we—"

"Why don't I just run you through the car wash again?" She pulled him toward her car.

She wasn't sure if he groaned with impatience or approval, but either way, she had a plan to show him how fun marriage could be.

She winked at him over her shoulder as she unlocked her car door. "Don't worry, I know from experience the pink bubbles are a real turn-on."

The Tennessee Ledger

Mating Season Open for Vanderbilt Students

NASHVILLE—Visiting professor Dr. Madeline Watson-Turner will speak on her popular book, *The Mating Season,* this Friday at 7:00 p.m. in the Vanderbilt auditorium. The lecture is open to the public and will include Dr. Watson-Turner's commentary on her extensive research in the area of human mating rituals.

Dr. Watson-Turner, a professor at the University of Louisville, is using the spring semester to tour campuses nationwide to discuss her *New York Times* bestseller. "Ever since *The Mating Season* hit the shelves, I've been inundated with questions regarding my research techniques for this study," she says. "I'm hoping the book tour will inspire other sociologists to tackle the projects of their dreams—even if they seem a little off the beaten path."

Certainly *The Mating Season* has been the kind of project dreams are made of for Dr. Watson-Turner. The book has gone into a fifth North American printing and is now in production overseas.

"I owe much of the book's success to my husband," Dr. Watson-Turner says of her entrepreneurial spouse, Cal Turner, who is in Nashville this week opening his twenty-fifth "Perfect Timing" business. "He's not only been a source of inspiration for me, he's left a lasting fingerprint on the canvas of my work."

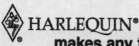

If you enjoyed what you just read,
then we've got an offer you can't resist!

Take 2 bestselling love stories FREE!

Plus get a FREE surprise gift!

Three of romance's most talented craftsmen come together in one special collection.

New York Times bestselling authors

Jayne Ann Krentz

Tess Gerritsen

National bestselling author

Stella Cameron

in

Stolen Memories

With plenty of page-turning passion and dramatic storytelling, this volume promises many memorable hours of reading enjoyment!

Coming to your favorite retail outlet in February 2002.

HARLEQUIN®

Makes any time special ®

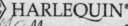